THE CATCH

THE CATCH

Prize winning stories by women

Edited by Carole Buchan

Library of Congress Catalog Card Number: 96–72580

A complete catalogue record for this book can
be obtained from the British Library on request

First published in 1997 by Serpent's Tail,
4 Blackstock Mews, London N4, and
180 Varick Street, 10th floor, New York, NY 10014
Website: www.serpentstail.com

Phototypeset in 10pt Sabon by Intype London Ltd
Printed in Great Britain by Mackays of Chatham plc, Chatham,
Kent

Contents

Foreword

A house in Sussex, once home to Virginia and Leonard Woolf, is the inspiration behind this collection of stories by women.

Asham House no longer exists, but its spirit lives on through the Asham Literary Endowment Trust, set up by Lewes District Council to support and encourage new writing and to celebrate literary excellence in all forms. In launching the first Asham Award, the Trust this year pays tribute to Virginia Woolf and to generations of women writers who have blazed a literary trail this century.

There is no common theme to this anthology, for it spans both time and continents to give a unique flavour of the exciting cultural diversity which is alive in Britain today, and the range of talent among the women writers of the nineties. Many of the award winners here are seeing their work in print for the first time, and their stories appear alongside those of five established women writers, including two Whitbread prizewinners.

I would like to thank Waterstones and the judges – Candia McWilliam, Rachel Cusk and Pete Ayrton of Serpent's Tail – for their enthusiasm and support for the Asham Award and for enabling the Trust to further its aim of giving a voice to the writers of tomorrow.

Carole Buchan,
Asham Literary Endowment Trust
Lewes, East Sussex

The Catch

Cari Crook

When Rattle first saw the pale hands scrabbling at the canal edge he was confused. Hands going under or hands trying to get out? There was no possibility of an answer. The whisky had him baffled.

He came to an unsteady halt and watched curiously. Whatever battle was going on, it was clear that the waggling white fingers were losing it.

Grass and black earth flew apart in the final struggle and then the cold little splashes, that had first attracted his attention, ceased.

Rattle took two shuffling steps off the towpath to look closer. The water was brown and impervious. Small pieces of canal bank – battle debris – swarm lazily round before sinking without protest.

"Well," said Rattle, liking the sound his voice made in the late afternoon's rawness. He cocked his head and listened. Down by the black hulk of the old factory, a dog barked huffily and from the darkening Recreational Ground, the last, ugly shouts of kids ripped through the dead air.

Rattle liked it here very much. It held an attraction for him. The very ground seemed to pull him to itself, so that he sat awkwardly down, his fingers tightening jealously round the neck of the whisky bottle.

"Hi."

The head had risen so smoothly, so quietly out of the canal, that Rattle was not unduly startled. He had seen funnier things after a bottle of whisky. At least it grinned at Rattle in a friendly way. It was a young face; the blue eyes decisively merry.

"I'm Pyke."

Rattle nodded. In the busy undergrowth behind him a bird thrashed and squawked desperately and then was silent.

Pyke had not stopped smiling, had not taken his bright blue eyes from Rattle's face. He pulled himself onto the bank with a single fluid movement. Like a beautiful shining, naked fish, thought Rattle.

Rattle, the scourge of all queers, real or imagined, found his mouth open and his heart skipping and prancing so that he could barely breathe.

Pyke remained on his hands and knees and shook himself like a dog. Bright droplets flew from him into the grey air. He peered at Rattle coyly, from under a slender, pale arm. "And you are?"

"Rattle," mumbled Rattle. He took a shaky swig from his bottle and then, wondering if he had been impolite, offered the bottle to Pyke.

Pyke grinned but shook his head. He yawned and stretched himself lazily beside Rattle. As if this was the Mediterranean and the sun was hot.

Rattle looked at him coyly, from under his lashes. Here and there, dark weed wound its way round Pyke, but he made no effort to brush it away. He did not seem to notice the glossy slug-like things that had attached themselves to him.

Rattle had seen those things before – had shrieked to Susie to shake them from the bed sheets before he got in. He wished that bitch were here now – then she'd see whether they were frigging real or not.

Something else began to worry Rattle. With an effort of will, which made his head ache unpleasantly, he brought it to mind.

"Sorry about you going in like that, mate." Had Pyke

realised that Rattle had watched him go under? Had not helped in any way? Would Pyke be angry about that? The thought of Pyke angry made him shiver fearfully and deliciously.

Pyke giggled and rolled onto his stomach. He ran a hand through his hair. It was reddish and curly. One of the slugs slapped onto the towpath. Pyke poked at it with a grey fingernail.

"But that wasn't me, Rattle."

Rattle watched the slug haul itself, quivering, off the towpath. It fell into the canal with a plop. God, he'd never have the bottle to touch those things. Nor would Susie. She just pretended they weren't there. She said the voices weren't there either. Wound him up something awful, she did.

Suddenly Rattle was confused. He felt sick. He thought that perhaps he didn't like this place after all; that, if he could only get up, he'd rather be in a nice warm pub somewhere, having a laugh with his mates.

Pyke leaned over and gave Rattle's knee a squeeze. Pain shot through Rattle; icy and ecstatic. He heard himself moan.

"This *is* where you belong. You know that really, Rattle, don't you?"

Rattle nodded helplessly. The pain was really unbearable. Pyke smiled and let him go. Rattle writhed and panted like a landed fish, until the pain, that stabbed between his knee and groin, subsided a little.

He opened his eyes. It was nearly dark now. Far away, on the edge of the industrial estate, the lights in the tower blocks began to shiver. He had lived there once. Did live there. He hugged his knees to himself and felt his eyes water in self-pity.

"She got what she deserved," remarked Pyke, chattily. "Women, what do you do with them, eh Rattle?"

For a second, Rattle thought he was talking about *her*, had somehow read his mind and found Susie squatting there. That little bitch Susie, who was probably nursing her bruises and her never-ending complaints down at the cop shop. Like she always did.

"Her that fell in. That's who you mean?" Rattle found it hard to get his tongue round the words. It felt thick and too big for his mouth. He tried again. "In the water. You mean it was a woman what fell in the water?"

Pyke gave a low laugh."Did she fall or was she pushed?"

Rattle blinked. The water was still. He didn't want to think about Susie.

Pyke had sat up. Rattle wondered why he had ever thought he was naked. He had a grey suit on, like those door-to-door religious nuts wore, only shinier, so that blues and greens danced off it like little scales.

On the bridge, the sodium lamp lit up the cycle track. Pyke was gazing into the light with a dreaminess and longing that made little tugs at Rattle's belly. His face was cast in yellow and there was a deep cold smell about him that Rattle had not noticed before.

But he knew it. It was how the drains smelt in the flats, except the plumber said they were fine. But Rattle had seen the way he and Susie looked at each other, like it was Rattle making it all up.

Pyke turned to him slowly. The yellow light had stayed in his eyes. Helpless troubled things swam in their depths.

"Time to tell me about that bitch Susie, Rattle."

Rattle could not take his eyes away from Pyke's. He thought he saw his own white face in them, his mouth a dark "O", as if he was shouting or screaming. He shivered.

"Cold, so cold," he moaned.

"It's that bitch Susie," observed Pyke. "That cold bitch Susie. It's her fault."

"Yes," said Rattle gratefully. "Her fault."

He could look away from Pyke now. Several icy stars hung in the sky. He drew a shuddering breath as more tears pricked his eyes. He thought of all the things he wanted to say about Susie.

"She laughed at me," he said at last.

Pyke tutted sympathetically while Rattle sobbed.

"She said they weren't real – said I was crazy."

"Of course they were real," said Pyke soothingly. "She was a lying bitch, Rattle. You did well to get rid of her." There was not a trace of accusation in his voice and Rattle had to agree. He had done the right thing. How could he have misunderstood it, forgotten it?

Suddenly Rattle saw her. Her white stilettos doing a frantic tap-dance on the canal's edge. Her tight little voice chipping away at him, all the while her red, taloned hands were scratching the air like claws. Only at the end did she shut up, the fear sagging her aggrieved pout at last, as one bleached leg slid away from her and down. And he was pushing her, one hand tense around her throat, caught on the cheap chain that always left green marks, that Susie never cared about, or noticed. It had driven him crazy. And his other hand, twisting her arm behind her, forcing her off her balance and down, until the black water lapped at the hem of her skirt.

Rattle jumped and looked around him. He felt as if he had been dropped from a great height and had just woken up. He reached for his bottle. It was empty,.

"Don't need that. Not now, Rattle – not where we're going."

"We're going somewhere?" Rattle looked at him uneasily. He was suddenly, horribly sober. He wanted another drink very badly. What had he told this neat-suited stranger sitting on the canal bank beside him? He couldn't remember. Then had a nasty thought. "You're not the frigging police are you?

Pyke laughed and shook his head. Rattle found he wasn't entirely relieved.

"Where then?"

Pyke pointed to the canal.

"Down there?" said Rattle stupidly. He peered at the black, impervious skin of water. There was nothing to see, no lights, no stars. When Pyke let his fingers stroke the water lovingly, there were no ripples.

"We fish down there," said Pyke dreamily.

"No fish in this canal – it's filthy." It was time to go home. Rattle tried to push himself up. Nothing happened. He gave a little grunt of surprise and fear.

Pyke put his face close to Rattle's and smiled. Rattle found himself looking at the sharp little bones that were Pyke's teeth. He felt the grey frigidity of Pyke's hissing breath.

"Look."

Rattle saw the empty bottle, half hidden by the undergrowth, and beside it a stiletto shoe. The shoe might have been white once, but now it was grey and moulded over with age and decay. A large, glossy slug wormed its way out of the toe.

At last, and too late, he thought he understood.

"Never meant . . ." he began, but he knew he had.

He took Pyke's scaly hand and then there was just the sinking and the swallowing.

The Dance

Leila Keys

From Mira to Ammu Madras
12th March 1974

Dear Ammu,

Last night, I dreamed of you. You are in a ship, sailing away. The night is dark, with neither moon nor stars, and I stand on the shore, cold and sad, watching the lights glimmer in the distance, and hear the swish of the sea. Then I see you on board, amid music, bright lights and laughter, and you are at a party. You are in your orange chiffon, with an orange hibiscus bright against your dark hair. I hear the throb of a guitar, the click of castanets. You are a flamenco dancer. But you are not dancing. You are standing, in a little group, the centre of it, and you are telling a joke. Like you often did, convulsed with laughter before the punch line, so that everyone laughed at your delight rather than at the joke, which was drowned in your squeals of laughter. But in the dream the joke is about me, and you are laughing at me, and so is everyone else. The dream then dissolves as dreams do, and I awake, feeling no resentment, but a great nostalgia for our times together. But that seems a very long time ago now.

It is now a year since you left for England, and it was no romantic ship that carried you off, only a Boeing 727 that was late, and we said a muddled goodbye at a crowded Madras airport, in the sticky heat of a March afternoon.

You looked nervous, almost frightened, and I envied you, for the excitement, the adventure ahead. At the foot of the steps before boarding, you turned and waved, and I felt your mother clutch my hand, and I sensed her soundless tears.

You have not written a word since then. I shall not know where to send this when I have written it. I suppose I could ask your mother for your address. Yet I am more than a little apprehensive about asking her, because I am afraid to find that she has not heard from you either, and doesn't know where you are.

It is perhaps fitting that I should dream of you and laughter, because that is how I and everyone else who knew you think of you, although there were those, including Vikram, who thought you were frivolous. Vikram, my husband, whom you have known as long as I have known him, and you, my best friend. Why should it have mattered so much that he said that?

Do you remember the evening he called you that? It was long past Saru's bedtime, and she was using every trick known to a four-year-old to avoid being sent to bed. Then there was the inevitable tantrum, and I was trying, ineffectually, to calm her down. I cajoled, I threatened. The screams got louder, and my exasperation near breaking point.

You had been stretched out on the settee, idly turning over the pages of a magazine. You put it down, and you got up and you danced, what you called your very own belly dance, for Saru, right in the middle of the living-room floor.

Vikram, who had been reading, quite oblivious to Saru's screams, put down his paper and watched. So did Saru, who hushed instantly, and stared open-mouthed at the vision of her favourite aunt, gyrating so gracefully for her benefit. She then crept into her father's lap. He put his arm round her and they watched together.

It was quite amazing. Your shoulders shook, your bosom

heaved, and through the single layer of your transparent sari, your navel, clearly visible between choli and skirt, quivered enchantingly. You clapped your hands and stamped your foot to the rhythm of your song without the slightest trace of self-consciousness. I realised what a perfect body you had, and what a lovely singing voice. The song and dance were supposed to be Spanish, your passion at the time, although they had clearly been made up, even perhaps on the spot. And yet, how on earth did you manage, in that repressive world we lived in? As I say, I was truly amazed.

I shall always remember that evening for another reason. I got a new insight into Vikram's so-called liberal attitudes. When you stopped, I clapped, and imitating me, Saru clapped too. I looked at Vikram, and I thought, "He is embarrassed."

He said nothing, picked up Saru, and took her to bed, perhaps for the first time that I can remember. When he came back, we were decorously seated, listening to a record of Spanish music.

He stood in the doorway and said, apropos of nothing, "Ammu, you really must stop being so frivolous, or you will never find a husband."

What was awful was that he did not say this with a smile. He looked completely serious, not a bit like the way he usually spoke, with warmth and affection even when he teased, which, as you know, was often. You somehow seemed to provoke, and enjoy, being teased, and I enjoyed the easy exchange of quick repartee between you.

I expected you to retort with something uniquely you, like, "and this is the thanks I get for stopping Saru's tantrum" or, "who wants a husband?"

Instead you burst into tears and left the room. When I tried to follow, you had locked your door, and would not answer.

I remember that evening so well, because after that I

saw you less and less. I could understand that you were hurt, and although I tried to visit you at your home, you were often out. Inevitably I saw more and more of your mother, who worried about you constantly, about what she called your irritability, and your impatience with her.

"What has got into Ammu?" she would ask me, and I began to think that you did not want my friendship any more. How could I have told her that? So I found other words of comfort. Although it is perhaps true to say that these visits gave me comfort, rather than the other way round.

"Mira," she said once, "you are so lucky. A nice husband, a beautiful child. What will become of Ammu if anything happens to me? A girl without a father, or even an uncle to arrange a marriage for her?"

And I would talk to her about your plans, to go abroad, become a lawyer, come back to India, go into politics. And she said impatiently one day, "Oh, Mira, I wish she would not be so frivolous." I did not tell you, did I? How could I? We hardly ever spoke. That night I told Vikram how unhappy I was, about the loss of my best friend, a loss that I considered he had been responsible for. He seemed genuinely surprised.

"Would you like me to talk to her?" he said.

"How would you do that?" I countered. "She hasn't been to see us for ages, and even I hardly ever see her. When I do, she has nothing to say to me at all."

"I know what," he said then, "I will write to her."

I didn't see the letter, but I believed him when he said he wrote it. As you know, it made no difference. You did not come to my home again, and you continued to avoid me.

So, when I said at the airport, "Ammu, write to me," and you said, "Of course," I knew you would not.

At the time, it was no more than wishing you would, and knowing you would not, because that is the way you had been with me for so many months. I was quite convinced that your life had moved on, and I had become domesticated and boring.

Then three months and five days ago, there was a sudden storm. The rain came down in deafening torrents. The windows rattled, with rumbling crashes of thunder. Warning flashes of lightning glinted back from the mirrors on the walls.

I went looking for Saru, who, as you know, is terrified of lightning. She was in Vikram's study, oblivious to the storm, and the thunder that would normally have sent her scurrying to me in fear. She had managed to get his desk open, and his papers were strewn all over the floor. Gathering them up to put them back, and struggling with her while she tried to snatch them back again, I hit upon the ruse of giving her an empty envelope to scribble on while I tidied up.

When I had finally got her to bed and to sleep, I came back to the study for a final clearing up. The envelope lay on the floor where we had dropped it, with Saru's scribble on it. She had drawn a house, with a door, and two windows, over and over again. As I was about to throw it into the wastepaper basket, I realised it was not empty. There was a single sheet of paper in it, and the handwriting unmistakably yours. You had written just four words. "It is a boy." The postmark was New Delhi, and that is where Vikram is tonight, on business.

I don't know how to end this letter. Perhaps my dream says it all.

Mira

From Vikram to Ammu Madras
15th March 1974

Dear Ammu,

Last night, I dreamed of Viswamitra. It was about you, of course. But then, as you used to say in the early days, I am never direct. When I have something to say, I usually tell a story, or quote from the Hindu texts: the point I would be trying to make, would invariably be self-serving, and dressed up in moral guise. You used to say all that with affection and teasing laughter, and I would laugh too, recognising a little truth in a great deal of exaggeration. But the last time we met, you said it with bitterness, your face furrowed and your fists clenched.

I fear I must tell you what I am going to say in my own way: I have no other. But before I tell you my dream, I must finish the story I started to tell you on that night my life fell so spectacularly apart.

That was such an extraordinary night. As I sat in the living-room in a trance, half asleep, you came down, and as though nothing at all had happened, as though I had not driven you out of the room in rage and embarrassment just a few hours before, you said, and I noticed that you did not look at me as you said it, that you had come to get yourself a book. You wore something soft, in pale green, that fell around you in folds, and I thought, "She sleeps in that."

I saw you through a haze of my own confusion, with blurred edges, and I was very much afraid that if I attempted to speak, there would be no sound. My mouth was dry, and I felt I could not breathe. Yet when I did speak, my voice sounded quite ordinary. With no sense then of the ridiculous inappropriateness of it, I started to tell you a story. The story of Viswamitra. You stood there, your arm raised to take down a book from the shelf, and looked at me with surprise, shaken momentarily out of your self-consciousness. You had been crying, and your hair fell about your face in disarray, and you looked so heartbreakingly young and bewildered, that I was completely, irretrievably, lost. I went on, knowing that with your Western education you had no idea who Viswamitra was, or what on earth I was talking about. But I told you only half the story. Or rather, my telling got interrupted halfway through.

Viswamitra, an ancient sage, having renounced the world, is in a deep trance in the depths of the forest. He is so still that birds nest in his matted hair, and anthills grow round him, and snakes burrow among them. Indira, King of the gods, feels threatened by the increasing spiritual power of this meditating ascetic. So he sends a dancer from his court, the beautiful Menaka, to tempt him. As Menaka dances, the music of her anklets disturbs Viswamitra, and he opens his eyes. And then, the dance. That has been described by a hundred poets down the centuries, and painted by as many artists. Viswamitra is utterly, helplessly, captivated. I watched you as I talked, and I knew you understood.

You put your book down, very gently, noiselessly, on the table, and stood very still, your loosened hair falling over your face, covering it completely. I came up to you then, took you gently by the shoulders, and as gently, swept the hair away from your face. It was like touching a rare and unfamiliar silk. I will never forget the magic of that moment. We did not talk much then, or you would have pointed out how presumptuous I was to liken myself to Viswamitra, or you, a budding lawyer, to the dancing temptress Menaka. And I would have remarked on the sadness of the fact that the British who gave us their language, which is rich, took away from us our culture that is richer. You would have then called me pedantic, or stuffy, which was more often the word you used for me. But what happened would not have happened, and you would not have needed to go away.

But as I said, I only told you half the Viswamitra story. He is completely besotted with Menaka, and breaks his vow of celibacy, to live with her in the forest. Then the predictable outcome, a baby, and the scene painted perhaps even more often than the dance of Menaka. Usually a pastoral scene, with a hut to convey domesticity, a stream, with grazing deer, flowers and blue skies. Then Menaka, now a mother, holding out her child to Viswamitra, who recoils, his head averted, his two palms extended to ward off the proffered gift. A classic pose of rejection, sung about down the centuries. The story ends with Menaka leaving the baby on a lotus leaf, and going back to Indira's court, while Viswamitra goes back to his meditation.

However, to come back to my dream of last night. I dreamed I was visiting my uncle in Hyderabad, who lives in rather a grand house, and collects old Indian paintings. From his hallway, a wide marble staircase sweeps up to the floor above, and on the landing, on either side of a large picture window, are the two Viswamitra pictures. To the left, the dance, and to the right, the rejection scene. In my dream, we, you and I, are climbing that staircase together. But when we come to the landing, the stairway suddenly stops, and the night sky surrounds us. There are stars above; below, the sound of rushing water, and ahead, a void of swirling blackness. I feel your hand tugging at mine, while I resist, fearful of the abyss below. Then you fall, or jump off. I hear a strangled cry, and it is my own, and even as I cry out, I know you fell because I released my hand from yours with more care for my own safety than yours. I wake up covered in sweat.

It is now four in the morning, at least another hour before dawn, and the house is silent. Mira has gone to visit her parents, and taken Saru. I was relieved on my return from Delhi to find them gone, to feel there was no need for enforced heartiness and the usual deception.

So we have a son. You would not let me see him, and I feel that is right, until I can think clearly of the future. You were right to be angry at my caution, and to point out that I had had plenty of time to think about it all.

In this letter I am trying to tell you that I have thought about it all, have thought about nothing else, these many months, and, in my usual roundabout way, I am trying to tell you the conclusion I have come to. However impatient you get with my indirect, ponderous ways of communicating my thoughts, you do in the end understand what I mean, and I feel sure you will now. You will be angry, but in the circumstances, that cannot be avoided.

Vikram

From Ammu to Vikram New Delhi
22nd March 1974

Dear Vikram,

I dreamed of you last night. You were writhing in agony at my feet, and I wore your entrails as garlands round my neck. My hands and face were smeared in blood. I carried a spear, and rode a fierce tiger, had fangs for teeth which were dripping with blood. Yours. Yes, I was Kali, the avenging goddess.

Well, I invented that dream, to show I could match you myth for myth. But I have no real stomach for it. I feel no rapport with Kali or Menaka and feel no great respect for Viswamitra whose piety threatened the King of the gods. Instead, I was much preoccupied with the baby left on the lotus leaf. What happened to it? Being myth, perhaps there was a friendly shepherd who was passing, and took care of it.

Coming back to my dream of the vengeful goddess, does it amuse you? Poor little Ammu, the disgraced unmarried mother, how could she take revenge? You do pity her, of course, but your duty is to your family. What can you do?

In the weeks and months when we seemed obsessed with each other, you made a number of rules. One of them was that we wrote no letters to each other, and if we did, they would be to impart information, no more. So these would have no prefix, no address, no signature.

When you wrote to me last you broke that rule. You called me Ammu, and signed yourself Vikram, and just before the end you acknowledged our son. I am no dancer from Indira's court, nor a cannibal goddess avid for blood. I am a lawyer, and you have put yourself completely in my hands. So the scope for revenge for little Ammu is considerable. I have no doubt you have a story to fit this situation. If you have, do let me have it.

Ammu

From Ammu to Mira New Delhi
12th December 1974

Dear Mira,

I dreamed of you last night. It was confused, full of ordinary domestic happenings, and you were there, being good and kind and sensible, as you always were, ever since I have known you. Ever reliable, but oh, so infuriating, because you seemed to get people to love you, so effortlessly, while I tried so hard. But somehow, it never quite worked for me. The dream made me sad, and perhaps just a little bit less bitter. I feel I owe you some form of explanation.

I wrote many letters, and tore them all up. Then I hit on the simplest way of telling you. I enclose Vikram's letter to me, and my reply, and these will tell you what I have so much difficulty bringing myself to say.

Perhaps I ought to add that I never did send my letter to Vikram. It is what I should have liked to say to him. I merely wrote it.

I shall send this packet of letters to my mother from whom you can collect it. I know you visit her often, and are, as she says, a great comfort to her. I am sure it is no secret to you that she has always wished that I was more like you, and less like myself.

Ammu

From Mira to Ammu Madras

21st June 1980

Dear Ammu,

I sat up with your mother last night. She has been very weak since her second stroke, and not always aware of her surroundings, but yesterday, around dusk, she opened her eyes, and seemed to see me, really see me.

I was holding her hand, and it felt responsive in mine, although she was so weak that she could hardly return my pressure.

She spoke in a whisper, and as I bent down to hear it, I smelt the talcum powder on her neck, and felt the soft cotton of her shawl brush my cheek. She wanted me to open the big wardrobe by the window, and it seemed she wanted her silver betel-nut box from it.

At first I thought she was wandering, and then I realised that the betel-nut box contained not betel leaf and nuts, but something else that she wanted me to see. I took it down, and took it to her. She waved it towards me, and when I tried to open it, she stayed my hand and whispered, "When you get home."

When I got home it was very late, and I sat alone on the flowered settee we had so often sat on together, and opened the casket discoloured with time. First, just under the lid, was a piece of paper, with your London address printed in block letters. I thought then that was what you mother had wanted me to have, as it was a matter of sadness for me that your mother had made it clear she did not wish to give me your address. Then, under a couple of layers of blank brown paper, I found my letter to you written six years ago. It had taken me a week after I had written it to bring myself to ask her for your address. She did not answer for a long time, and as I was beginning to wonder whether she had heard me, she said, with an uncharacteristic vagueness: "I have it around somewhere. You give me your letter, and I will send it on."

Her tone did not brook discussion or argument. And I gave her my letter, which, as I say, was in the box. After that it became curiously difficult to talk about you. I think we tacitly hit upon a formula that worked reasonably well.

"Heard from Ammu?" I would ask, knowing that she would answer, "No, not for some weeks." And that was all. It does not matter now, as that letter has long since become irrelevant.

But there was more in this treasure trove of a betel-nut box. Under further layers of blank brown paper was your packet addressed to me, enclosing your letter to me, Vikram's to you and yours to him which you did not send. They were all there, these letters we wrote to one another. Your mother had kept them all.

I have been to see her this morning, and she seemed to be at peace. She told me then, her whisper getting stronger and clearer as she spoke, that you were happy, married to a barrister in London, and that he knew all about your little daughter, and has adopted her.

"A daughter?" I said in astonishment, and then realised that was your revenge. Vikram fretting for a son he could not see, a son I was not able to give him.

Last week was parents' evening in Saru's school, and Saru gave her first Bharathanatyam dance recital. She was Menaka. A ten-year-old Menaka, she played all the parts with consummate skill: the seductress, the mother, the rejected mistress, unfazed at her rejection, off to where she belonged, in Indira's court, with her mission accomplished.

Saru's innocent ten-year-old face was brilliantly expressive, her eyes triumphant, pleading, resigned, her hands and her head articulate, first as Menaka, and then, severe, as Viswamitra, dignified even when he is tempted and falls, and then angry, magnificent in his sense of outrage, that she should have dared to seduce him, the powerful sage feared by the gods.

But what, you ask in your undelivered letter to Vikram, of that baby that was left on the lotus leaf? Alas! that formed no part of the recital. But I can tell you what happened in the myth. It was a baby girl, and she was called Shakuntala, who was later wooed by Prince Dushyanth, and they had a son, called Bharath, the first great king of India, India being really Bharath in all the Indian languages.

So you see, your daughter, whom I shall think of as Shakuntala, will have a glorious future.

Mira

Inner Balance

Kate Atkinson

June. If she'd been born in November would they have called her November? She asked her mother this once. *Oh, June, you are funny.* June. It's a name for women in sitcoms and soaps, the name of women who knit with synthetic wool and follow recipes that use cornflakes. Nice people. June doesn't want to be nice people. June gets her nose pierced and wears a little ruby in the hole like a pinprick of blood. *At your age!* June's mother says.

The name doesn't belong to June, it belongs to her mother. *It's amazing, isn't it*, says June (the mother), *that we were born in the same month?* Not really, thinks June (the daughter), not given that there are only twelve months in the year and millions of people being born all the time. Thinks it betrays a serious lack of imagination not to be able to see further than your own name when christening another person. June.

June's parents – Ian and June senior. Old and stupid. And nervous – they're nervous about everything, from being mugged on the way home from the post office with their pensions to dying of carbon monoxide poisoning. Their lives are peppered with alarms – carbon monoxide alarms, smoke alarms, burglar alarms, car alarms – her mother even has a personal alarm ("in case I'm raped, dear") that she carries everywhere with her in her dreadful old handbag where it nestles amongst half-used Kleenex and packets of Rennies. They're alarmed, June thinks to herself and laughs out loud. Their white hair and their nerves remind June of sheep. When she closes her eyes and thinks about them (which she tries not to do but often does) she sees sheep in brown anoraks and Gore-tex.

They were old when they had June. *Our one and only* says June the elder. June (forty-three) and Ian (forty-five) when they had June (nought). June doesn't know how they did it, she's only thirty-five but already she feels far too worn out to have another baby. She wouldn't want another baby – even if it was Mr McFarlane's. June's waiting for her parents to die so she can grow up and stop behaving badly. Whenever she goes near them she regresses twenty years. *You're a funny one* her mother says, but you can see she's not really laughing.

June – that's it, you can't do anything with it, can't lengthen it to Junie (sounds like chewing-gum) or shorten it to Ju. Unless you were Chinese perhaps. June is not Chinese, she's Scottish. From Perth.

"Pairrth," says Mr McFarlane in his lovely douce Aberdonian. "That's a bonny place."

"Is it?" June says grumpily. They wait for their appointment with him in the E.N.T. waiting-room, which is really a corridor. "Ent," says Alistair, reading a sign, his little face pinched and adenoidal. "Not 'Ent'," June corrects him, "E-N-T – ear, nose and throat." Two years they've been coming here and this is the first time he's asked what it means. First time she's thought to tell him. What does he say to his teacher when he gives her a note – "I have to go to the ent clinic." Surely not. "What?" he says. "E-N-T," June spells out, her lips making exaggerated shapes. "Are you waiting for Mr McFarlane?" a neat chirpy nurse says to Alistair, but he's looking at the watch pinned to her chest and misses what she says. Half the world passes him by. June wishes something would pass her by, wishes everything would pass her by. She'd like to sleep for a long time and be woken up with a kiss from Mr McFarlane and feel his pale, soft fingers touching her cheek the way they touch Alistair's when he's peering through his auriscope.

June is waiting for Mr McFarlane. She's waiting to marry him. She's waiting for the first Mrs McFarlane to die or fall in love with someone else – preferably the latter option, then June wouldn't have to bring up Mr McFarlane's children.

"Hello there, Alistair," Mr McFarlane says. "And how are you today?" One day, June thinks, she will open the door of their flat in Newington and Mr McFarlane will be standing there, slightly out of breath from the four flights, and he'll say – but what will he say? What is it that June wants him to say?

Mr McFarlane sits Alistair up on his desk and peers into his left ear. June wishes he would do something this intimate with her, look inside her brain with his little torch and see how lonely she is. On a table in the corner Mr McFarlane has a model of the inside of a giant's ear. The ear's almost as big as Alistair and coloured in shades of pink and blue. The ear comes to pieces and Mr McFarlane usually spends most of their appointment deconstructing and reconstructing it with Alistair. Sometimes June has a vision of the future, where the grown-up Alistair knows nothing about history or maths or geography or anything useful, but can take people's ears apart. You can tell just by looking at Mr McFarlane, peering through his spectacles and fiddling with the hammer and anvil bones of the giant's ear, that his boyhood was spent building working Meccano models and gluing Airfix kits together. June has a great fondness for the childhood she imagines for Mr McFarlane. She would like this childhood for Alistair. If she married Mr McFarlane then perhaps she would be able to give this childhood to him. Alistair spends his time lost in his own private world of the half-deaf. June imagines it's like being on the ocean floor listening to someone shouting down to you through the muffled boom and crash of waves and swells. "The organs of Corti," says Mr McFarlane mysteriously.

Mr McFarlane sits down in his chair and looks at the

results of Alistair's latest hearing test. Mr McFarlane's lips move when he reads the same way that Alistair's do. June's heart reaches out to Mr McFarlane. He has dreadful shoes, always the same shoes – black slip-on moccasins that need polishing. That need throwing away really. June wonders what kind of a wife lets a man wear shoes like that. If June was Mrs McFarlane she would make him buy new shoes. Today he has on Argyle socks, patterned in blue and green, and old grey flannel trousers like a schoolboy's. Over everything he wears his creased white overcoat that makes him look like a lab assistant pretending to be a consultant. He has dark hair that's thinning and cheap wire-rimmed glasses that make his eyes look enormous. His eyes are the colour of the Water of Leith, grey and dirty, but full of compassion for everything from Alistair's scarred eardrums to the thread coming loose from the rainbow sleeve of June's jumper.

"That's nice," he says pointing at the band round her thin wrist and June blushes hot and rosy with pleasure and says, "It's a friendship bracelet, I make them." She wants to say, "I'll make one for you, if you'd like," she'd like to offer him the gift of her friendship (really she'd just like to offer herself), but she doesn't have the nerve and instead says, "I sell them, I've got a stall in the Grassmarket during the festival."

"Ah," he says, as if this somehow explains everything.

The huge cochlea on the model ear is whorled like a shell and coloured in pale blue, a delicate colour like the sky over the Forth in February. Like today. June thinks of Alistair's cochlea as being blue, a fragile piece of sky furled inside his skull. Mr McFarlane has said that sometimes problems with the inner ear can have emotional causes, but June doesn't want to think too much about that.

"Are you doing anything nice at the weekend, Alistair?" Mr McFarlane asks. Alistair experiences a kind of time delay while he unscrambles language. "Yes," he says, "we're going to Gran's."

*

Alistair trails behind June like a limp flag, all the way up the four flights of their tenement. The cast-iron staircase turns like a stretched cochlea, like one of Alistair's shells unwound. June tells herself not to think like this all the time. It's like when she did the shorthand and typing course – all the time translating what people were saying into shorthand, little squiggly Pitman hieroglyphics running in front of her eyes like cartoon men. Now she's obsessed with ears. "Here we are," she says unnecessarily as she turns the key in the lock.

"I've got to stop smoking if I want to get up those stairs," she says sinking into an armchair and making a spindly roll-up – biting her lower lip intently like someone making a bomb. "What?" Alistair says, from the bottom of the ocean.

"Nothing."

Over tea, Alistair asks, "Are we going to Gran's tomorrow?" and June says, "Yes-for-the-hundredth-time." Alistair plays with his food, building a fort out of field beans, a moat full of white tofu. "I hate this food," he says. "It's good for you, it's macrobiotic," June says, fingering the coloured weaving on her friendship bracelet. After tea, Alistair plays with his shells, he calls it a collection, tracing the whorls and spirals with his finger and sorting them by size. It's not a collection really, just a few shells he picked up when they lived on the West Coast. "In a caravan?" Mr McFarlane asks doubtfully. "Yeah," June says, "why not?" but she says it nicely, not like she does to her mother. "But now you're living in Newington," he smiles, looking at the address on the top of Alistair's records. "Yes," June says. "It's got a nice view, you can see Arthur's Seat."

"That's lovely," Mr McFarlane smiles. It's a lie, they can see the back of an old warehouse. But if you climbed up on the roof you could see Arthur's Seat.

Alistair starts reading his shell book, his lips moving silently. It's an old book they found on a second-hand stall – *The Encyclopaedia of Conchology* – and Alistair likes to recite the names of shells in his head like some kind of spell, *Abida, Abra, Absia*. June gets ready to go out. She's going to classes in polarity therapy at the Salisbury Centre. She's done T'ai chi and hatha yoga and meditation. She's working towards being a real person, balanced and healthy. Wholesome. June imagines Mr McFarlane leads a wholesome life – not a smoker, definitely not. And not a drinker – maybe a glass of wine with a meal now and then. Imagines him driving out to Musselburgh at the weekends and walking his dog along the banks of the Esk. For his dog, June imagines a Labrador – chocolate-coloured and friendly and very obedient.

June used to do a lot of drugs, nothing hard, nothing you would have to inject. June hates injections. When she was thirteen and had a TB jab at school she got so hysterical that they had to call for her mother. June the first hovering in the sick-room of Perth Academy looking small and indefinite (*Oh June, you are a one*) making June the second even more hysterical. June hasn't done any drugs for a long time, except for the odd joint now and then, not since she left Alistair in his buggy alongside the disposable nappy aisle in Boots' in Princes Street and was on the bus going over the South Bridge when she remembered him. Now she's cleaning away all the bad stuff. Imagines filling her head with sky. "Come on," she says to Alistair, handing him his rainbow scarf (June knits everything the same – in thin stripes of any-colour-going), "you have to stay with Lianne."

"I don't want to go to Lianne's," Alistair grumbles, snailing behind her on pavements slick with rain, and June feels a guilty little clutch at her heart for his powerlessness.

She's not got rid of all the bad stuff inside her head yet though. Sometimes she gets a rage, not one that's hot and red with passion, but cold and blue with meanness, and Alistair disappears into his bedroom and fingers his shells like talismans and recites his mantras, *Nicania, Neverita, Nisso*. Then June gets even madder and meaner and tells him to stop or he'll end up in the loony bin. Then she feels guilty and June doesn't like feeling guilty so she gets even meaner, spiralling down the mean, blue labyrinth until she feels so bad that she thinks they would be better off if they were dead – if she smothered Alistair with a pillow in the night and then dived off the windowsill – but she couldn't do that. Not really. But it's an idea.

When she's got rid of this nastiness, June thinks, when she's balanced and her head's full of sky, she's going to invite Mr McFarlane up to the flat. Cook him a nice meal – stir-fry and brown rice – and show him all the best things about herself. Then he'll never go back to his wife, he'll stay with June and she'll knit him jumpers and buy him shoes and get him a chocolate-coloured Labrador. "We are going to Gran's, aren't we?" Alistair asks again, his voice muffled in rainbow scarf.

"Sit down, sit down," June's mother fusses round the tea-table nervously. Brought up in the meat-and-two-veg school of cuisine, June senior never knows what to feed them when they come to visit. Usually she just trawls the shelves of Marks and Spencer's food hall for something with a big green "V" on it. Alistair picks up his knife and fork before there's anything on the table. "Come on, father," June's mother says and June's father smiles and says, "All right, mother," and shambles to the table. June glares at them both. "Cheers," June's father says, raising a glass of lemonade. June feels about fourteen years old. Why don't they just die? They won't though, will they? They'll go on getting older and older. They'll probably outlive June. And if not, then it won't be long before things start going wrong with them, they already complain about arthritis, rheumatism, stiffness, bunions. Their eyes, ears, teeth and toenails. Soon it'll be the big stuff, their bladders, their brains. "Aye," June's mother says, "old age disnae come by itsel." A real old wifie. June will never grow like her mother. Never, ever, ever.

Soon, June knows, they're going to try hauling her in by the umbilical cord, she'll have to deal with their incontinence and their amnesia, she'll have to listen to endless tales about malfunctioning bowels and intimate female parts that she can't believe her mother really has. This is their fault, she thinks, stabbing a slice of potato. "Leek and Potato Bake," June's mother says like an advert (although not one that would encourage you to buy anything). This is their fault for only having one child. Only child, June thinks, that's the worst thing in the world to be. An only, lonely child. It's wicked to do that to someone, not to give them brothers and sisters. June catches the eye of her own only, lonely child and winces. June's mother gets up from the table and comes back in with a transparent plastic mould. "Trifle," she beams at Alistair. June reaches across and takes the lid off and reads the ingredients written on it. June's mother has already dolloped out a big red, yellow and white quivering spoonful into Alistair's bowl. He smiles happily. "Gelatine," June announces sternly. "It's got gelatine in it."

"Is that bad, dear?" June's mother asks tremulously, the spoon hovering over the remaining trifle. "Of course it's bad," June snaps, "it's made from boiled-down cows' bones and hoofs and other bits too disgusting to think about. Things swept up off abattoir floors probably."

"June," June's father remonstrates gently.

"He can't have it," June says. "Give me the bowl, Alistair." Alistair pushes his bowl across to June and stares at the space left on the tablecloth. His lips move, trembling slightly as he recites to himself – *Turbinella spirilis, Ensatella, Lucidella, Purpurifera* – like exotic girls' names.

"Banana then, dear?" June's mother says to him, sounding as if she's about to burst into tears. Then, June thinks, they'll go into a nursing-home and the DSS will sell their house from under them to pay the fees and June will have put in thirty-five years as their daughter and have nothing to show for it, not even this solid pink sandstone house. She would like to live here. Without them, of course. A real home, with a garden, a view of the hills, the Tay. If they died now, she'd get it all, the house, the insurance policies, their "little nest-egg". Why don't they die? Alistair eats his banana miserably. June imagines killing her parents. Spicing their bedtime Horlicks with aconite, splicing their smokies with cyanide. Maybe she could get a gun and just shoot them. That would be satisfying. June sees herself blowing their wobbly grey heads off, splattering blood over the Sanderson wallpaper. "Cuppie, dear?" June's mother says, lifting the teapot for June's inspection. "No milk," June says sullenly. "That's what makes veal calves."

"Oh dear," June's mother says. "I've never had veal."

June sleeps in her old bedroom, Alistair in the "guest room". June doesn't know why it's called that, they never have guests staying over. They have hardly any friends. Just each other. That's what June's father says, "We've got each other, that's all we need." And June, of course, they've got June. June's bedroom has been preserved as if she was dead. A shrine to her dead childhood. It's pink, everything's pink, the sprigged curtains, the bedspread, even the carpet blooms with pink roses. On a kist in the corner her Sindy doll sits pertly in a pink ballgown, her teddy-bear lolls his old head on a blue rabbit's shoulder. June huddles under her pink bedspread and pink cellular blankets and tries to switch her brain off. The worst thing is that she feels so safe here, under the pink covers, inside the pink sandstone. This is where she feels at home. It's horrible. She thinks about Mr McFarlane, imagines the kind of house they would live in if they got married. Solid and square, rooms with high ceilings and picture-rails. Imagines Mr McFarlane climbing into their big double bed with an expensive orthopaedic mattress. Mr McFarlane will wear pyjamas. He'll put his arms round June and say, what will he say? He'll say, *Don't worry, June, I'll look after you*. Yes, that's what June wants him to say. June wants somebody to look after her.

June falls asleep in the shelter of the pink house, in her safe childhood bed. She dreams she's standing at the living-room window in Newington. There's a line of bright blue snails crawling along the window-sill and from the window you can see Arthur's Seat, in fact, the window is full of Arthur's Seat, like a blind that's been pulled down on the outside. And the green grass is covered with little pink flowers and in the dream June thinks, *Oh good, now I can show Mr McFarlane*.

The Velvet Maid

Anne Summerfield

The room, *my* room, is narrow, whitewashed, sparsely furnished. There is a brass bed, scarcely bigger than a baby's cot, a wall cupboard for my clothes, a vivid stripe of window. The curtains and bed cover are made of cheap printed cotton, a block-printed pattern once china blue but now worn so thin that it is a mere shadow on a greyish ground. The bowl and jug placed on the floor are of dented enamel pricked with spots of rust. At some time the room must have been divided, and this, the less fortunate part, lacks the fireplace and chimney that must lie somewhere beyond the boarding. In early evening, the room is already chill.

I will not have to work here, of course. In honour of the importance of my task, the most senior dressmaker has been moved and I am to have her workroom. The keys to that room clank heavily on the chain the housekeeper hands over. And then the housekeeper leaves me alone, in the first room I have ever had for my own. Madame Labanne's teaching had not covered this aspect of my life. "Each house will be different," Madame always claimed. "There is nothing I can teach, but that you should keep your five wits about you."

So I am unprepared for the emptiness of the single room, a thin wall away from the chatter of the other servants. And in the morning I am equally unprepared to be woken by the sound of the others rising to a morning as dark as it is cold, to hear the second parlour maid battle with her bonnet, as the fruit chef curses stains on her apron where juice has splashed from rhubarb leaves, while the calico maid examines burn marks on her hands and despairs.

Like many of the girls trained at Madame Labanne's I had never chosen to be a velvet maid. It was a choice made for me, perhaps by Mother. I preferred to think it was the choice of the man who had once been my Father. Mother would not speak of him, lest it hurt her husband's pride, but I always felt Father had a part in the decision. But once that decision was made, there could be no return. The coast track between school and my village, inaccessible in winter except to the strongest and bravest fell pony, made travelling an impossibility. So I had been allowed to sleep in a corner of Madame Labanne's velvet workshop. My dreams, like my days, had been littered with fraying scraps of velvet: orange velvet the colour of tiger lilies, faded mud-brown velvet, gold corn-ear velvet, scarlet velvet thick as blood, moss-green velvet for breeches, grey-blue like rain clouds, vibrant mustard yellow, wild rabbit grey, pink raspberry fool, purple as damson skin wet with dew and heavy with bloom.

Alone in the tiny room which seems more than ever to have been bleached of all colour, I dress carefully in my white muslin gown. I tie back my hair with trembling fingers and for the first time cover it in a soft white snood trimmed with the single blue ribbon of velvet – sign of my trade. I cover my disobedient fingers in my long cotton gloves, collect my sewing basket and go to meet the dressmaker at eight when she will bring the calico replica, a milk-yellow imitation already designed, cut and fitted, of the dress I must transform into a wedding gown of ivory silk velvet.

"It seems so early in the autumn to use velvet," the dressmaker sniffs. "A nice thick moire taffeta would have been just as warm and even more luxurious." She shows me the garment resting on the headless calico form shaped as Miss Alicia. "You have one week," she says, staring at the scuffed toes of my boots. "All fabric trimmings must be returned to me. Other houses may be extravagant with their waste. Here at Redwings we are more frugal." Then she leaves me to my work, snapping the door closed. The workroom will be for my sole use, and she will be forced to complete the bridesmaids' dresses in the tiny box room where she sleeps.

As soon as the dressmaker leaves I open the parcel of velvet. It has been bundled in thick brown paper and specially imported to Redwings. I cut the tight rope surrounding the package and watch the velvet spring free, spilling and frothing like milk from the churn. The dark, scratched wood of the table is covered in white, sparkling white like sunlit snow. Colours ripple through it where it folds. I smooth it flat with my gloved hand, yet still the greys and creams, apricots and lemons play over the surface. Images flicker over the weft, resonances like melodies half formed. Mythical beasts with heads of lions and bodies covered in scales chase horned dolphins through hoops of fire. Quickly, I turn away.

I set to work sketching the finished gown, then unpick its seams to create the pattern pieces I need. I work rapidly, but the design is complex. The dressmaker, knowing she would not have to sew the final garment, included many tiny difficulties of detail – fine corded loops for buttons, piped edging for cuffs, a hidden placket fastening which must be implanted in a curved seam. The work is made harder by the strength of the dressmaker's stitches, which tear at the fine gauze of the fabric when I try to remove them. I absorb myself in activity but still I am drawn back to stare in the whirlpool of the velvet's surface. It is the most beautiful thing I have ever seen, this smooth, white emptiness. I do not want to change it at all. It is too hard, too painful to begin. I want to leave Redwings and go back to my mother's farm and pull turnips with my bare hands until they bleed. I have never been more afraid.

In the sewing room the velvet lies luminous across the

room like a shaft of moonlight, a moonbeam fallen to earth. The pictures begin again. Faces leaning large into mine, smiles like lanterns. I see shepherd's purse being picked by my baby hand, held aloft and rattled. I blow the dandelion clock and watch the angels float up into the sunlight. For a long time all I can do is stare deep into the fabric. I feel that I can never touch it again. I must not look at its surface, must not allow myself to be drawn in. And then I see her. Madame Labanne, dressed in her impossible patchwork of ancient silk velvet from Genoa and Spitalfields, Madame with her long waving grey hair and her face as round as a pumpkin, her voice soft and sensuous but insistent. "You must," says Madame's voice. "First you must straighten the grain and press the fabric." In the borrowed room, Madame's voice echoes as I tug at a leading thread to guide me to the grain.

"To press velvet you will need a velvet board, a sleeve pad (also of velvet), a warmed iron, a dampened muslin cloth and a light touch. Before you start you must check that the pile has meshed perfectly with the pile of the velvet board. Lower it gently in place so that the two sets of velvet teeth bite perfectly. Without this you could be pressing on linen or hessian for all the use of the velvet board. The two velvets together must create a thick layer of air, trapped in the fibres. It is this air which will save the pile.

"And like mixing a soufflé, your touch is essential. It is easy to beat out the air, to work too fast and to flatten. Like your soufflé, you may not see the damage of the wrong touch straight away, but once a velvet is worn, a velvet with the air beaten out, then the damage will show too well. The pile will be ruffled, the sheen gone, the hang of the fabric will be ruined. And once you have a flat velvet, it is as useless as a flat soufflé, fit for nothing except the pigs."

Madame's face smiles up at me from the smooth shimmering fabric. It is the end of my first day's work.

Cutting the velvet is the most frightening part, the first

cut the worst of all. The hand must be steady, unfaltering. It seems impossible, but I must go on. I dress specially that morning: two pairs of pantaloons, a thick camisole, muslin slippers for my feet, fine gloves for my hands. Over these I place my ordinary day clothes, long muslin gown, house shoes, snood and thicker gloves.

On the long table there are two lengths of edge-to-edge velvet, piles locked. I roll out the muslin pattern pieces and drop them in place. No pins, this is part of the skill, as the fewer holes made in the fabric the better. Instead the pattern is held softly by its own weight.

I remove my day clothes and climb onto the table. The muslin slippers are spotless, washed repeatedly for cleanliness and for grip. From my basket I take the long, cruel knife, a gift from Madame Labanne. On the handle my name in stones, Emily.

With the knife I carve the pattern shapes from the velvet, holding the fabric in place with my feet, moving and weaving a complex dance over the table. I hum the songs we were taught, songs that subdue and calm the velvet, songs that work like spells to keep the hand steady and the knife sharp. The fabric yields and glows as the knife blade flashes needles of light.

I work until the room grows dark, and night comes early in the form of a storm. The velvet pieces are spread flat round the room, an irregular patchwork. They are bright puddles in the darkening room. I put away my knife, put on my dress and day shoes. The velvet sings a soft goodnight.

To pin the velvet I use fine needles, not pins. It is slower, of course, far more difficult, but it is the only way to prevent marks on the fabric. Tacking must be done with fine silk thread. All day I work for as long as there is sunlight, and late at night I am still tacking by the glow of a candle. My gloves hinder me, but I have to wear them. They can only be removed for the final stage.

It is not my place to do the fitting. The dress is taken from me by a housemaid and carried brusquely to Miss

Alicia's bedchamber. The housekeeper brings me garments to repair while I sit alone and wait. There is a black velvet cape with tangled pile, an emerald dress, creased and smelling sour with sweat, a crumpled turquoise waistcoat ridged where the buttons pulled too tight, a cream embroidered cummerbund with unravelled stitching. Each must be steamed, cleaned, pressed. I work hard but I still rejoice when the wedding gown is returned at last.

"You may begin stitching," the housemaid instructs. "The fit is adequate."

I take my finest needle and silk thread. At last I can pull off the gloves and touch the fabric with my naked fingertips. And I begin to stitch.

I sew myself into the fabric, for I know no other way. The days with my mother picking raspberries in the cottage garden go into the sleeves. My first toddling steps carrying my "baby" – a wooden peg wrapped in scraps – are anchored in the high wings of the collar. My first childish kiss, tasting of sour green windfalls, slips into the curve of the waist band. The skirt takes the smell of the surf and the crash of the tides. My whole life passes through my fingers into the silken threads.

But each stitch costs. Each sinew used, tiny muscles of the hand pulling tiny knots of bone, each bears the burden. In time joints will swell and seize. I remember Madame's hands, gnarled and rigid, more tree root than flesh. The needle works through the fabric as softly as breathing, in, out, in, out. The time indoors fades the cheeks and dulls the skin, the senses become blunt to larger movements and focus on the slow movement of the silver needle and its snail trail of stitches. Time is nipped into seam-sized lengths.

Suddenly it is complete, a body shaped in glowing fabric. I find threads to neaten, tiny, almost invisible, bits of lint to flick away. The dress slides onto its form and it is of me but not me. It has taken my life and made a life of its own, and I am left bereft looking at it blissfully glowing. I am transfixed, detached and yet it is my work. Where did it come from? It has risen up from the shards that surround the form like confetti.

I bend to pick up the scraps. Each velvet piece cries out to be stroked and I do not resist, running my forefingers up and down. Down the fabric is sleek, slippery smooth, bright as knives. Up it is darker, more mysterious, a thick soft forest of dense undergrowth, dragging against my fingers. I love the jagged edges of cut velvet, the way that it frays in tiny crinkled fingers. I pick at the edges and take the threads into my mouth, tickle them against my tongue. The velvet tastes like salt when you lick it down, like seal pelt slicked in place by icy oceans. Licked upwards it is creamier, rich dark chocolate, cloying. The threads are spun from praline, buttery and splinteringly fragile. My gloved fingers are warm, sticky with the sweet, sour, brittle stuff. I cram those fingers into my mouth and suck my life back.

The dressmaker strides in, looking for tell-tale snippets and threads that she can complain about. She collects the brown paper bundle of scraps I have packaged, bustling it under her arm. "You will not need the key again," she says. "Perhaps it would be best to return it now." And she extends her bare, chafed hand. I glance across at the dress and know she will not resist following my gaze, then I watch her face change as her eyes come to rest on its pearly whiteness. Her face flickers as she refuses to smile. "I will leave you to your work now." Her jaw is as rigid as wish-bone. I wish, I wish. Snap. She turns to walk away.

"If you can make velvet patchwork then you can make almost any garment," Madame claimed. We maids struggled with the tiny squares, diamonds and triangles of slippery fabric, pricking fingers with needles deflected by the shining pile. Madame would shriek at us to keep our fingers away, as the scarlet drops began to form, bulging close to the scraps of fabric. "It will be ruined, ruined by blood," Madame said. "Never will you remove such a stain completely."

For my apprentice piece I made a dress of patchwork

velvet like Madame's own. The dress is long, black, slim fitting. I will carry it to each house where I work. That dress is my reference, the proof of my craft. It is not a dress meant to be worn, but I know that it fits me more than adequately.

Ami de Maison

Julia Widdows

It was July when he moved into Kilmartin Road, and the plane trees with their speckled bark were in full leaf. Kilmartin Road was not very long, hardly more than two hundred yards, and it led from the High Street at one end to a warren of nondescript residential roads at the other, named after vaguely Irish connections, or ancient Greek ones, Agamemnon Street being the most memorable. Kilmartin Road divided up into two distinct areas, his flat being in a house on the wrong, or less desirable, side of the street. On his side the houses were tall, flat-faced, the stucco painted in job-lot, bargain-basement colours like lilac, or khaki, or battleship grey. There were outside pipes that were plainly leaking, and occasional windows where the glass had been replaced by cardboard, and the tiny front gardens were mostly concrete or grim crazy paving, and piled with dented dustbins or black plastic bags. But in front there were the plane trees, as tall as the houses, probably the same age; and the morning sun shone into his rooms, and he was perched up on the first floor, airy and high.

Across the road was a terrace of Edwardian houses, two storeys only, built of red brick with white trimmings, solidly pilastered and windowed and arched, with tended front gardens, and paths of chequered tile, and wrought-iron gates that actually shut. They were family houses, whereas on his side the tall terraces were divided into flats, and even, judging by the look of some of the occupants, ramshackle bedsits.

That autumn was mild and wet and the big plane leaves stayed on the trees, giving his rooms a feeling of the countryside, and privacy, that he didn't look forward to losing. Then, towards the end of October, just as the clocks were being put back, there came three or four days of fierce winds, followed by a sudden sharp frost, and when it was over the only leaves left on the trees were right at the ends of the uppermost branches, like little pennants, wagging in the wind. And even then the leaves that had fallen were mainly bright green, or the colour of lemon peel, or at most a light golden brown, like roast potatoes. And all the size of plates – tea plates, dessert plates, even dinner plates. His eye, as he walked down Kilmartin Road, scanned to find the biggest – and yet bigger – leaves upon the pavement and in the gutter between the parked cars. He longed to pick up the biggest he could find and take it home. That would *be* an autumn leaf. If he were a family man, he could legitimately pick up leaves and carry them home, because people would think he was taking them home to his child. But as it was, he had no excuse, and left the beautiful things there to rot, and went indoors.

Until the leaves fell from the trees he had scarcely noticed the house across the street. Once, in summer, he had come down the road, on the opposite pavement, as if associating himself with the redbrick, decent, family side of the road and not the reprobate, scruffy, disenfranchised side; and he saw ahead a bunch of coloured balloons bobbing in and out of a gateway. He crossed to his own side, and looking back, saw that there were more balloons beneath the archway, attached to the letterbox of the solid black front door. Later that afternoon he was aware of much traffic on the pavement, of children being fetched by parents from a party, children laden with balloons, and cardigans, and bags of sweets, things too numerous almost to hold. He noticed them because the mothers – it was mostly mothers

– and occasional fathers hung about, standing at the gateway and straggling down the street, talking and calling to one another as if they could hardly bear to go. But apart from that one occasion, when he looked out, he looked out into the leaves.

It was almost dark now when he came home from work, and the windows of Kilmartin Road were lighted, many of them on the redbrick side, and a few, here and there, like odd portholes in a tall ocean-going liner, high up on his side of the road. The house across, he noticed from his living-room, had a music stand in the window of the downstairs front room, where the curtains were still pushed back. And he could see an elbow, the elbow of a child, and the neck of a violin with its whorled end. It reminded him of when he had practised his violin as a boy, and he went and put on a tape of the Bach double violin concerto, and thought what a civilised life he now lived.

The house across the road, he saw, used its first floor front room as a sitting-room. He could see an apricot-coloured rug – or it looked apricot in the gentle lamplight – and pale polished floorboards. There was a chaise longue with a curled mahogany end, covered in whitish fabric. And after a while it disappeared, and then came back in the same place, upholstered in a rich, striped, coral-coloured material. Someone in that house was clever, had reupholstered it, for he never saw the piece of furniture going in or out of the house. And he had been here, for a whole week, struck down by a bout of flu.

Since the summer his office life had become somehow less rewarding. Two of his colleagues had gone, one to Sheffield to be with his girlfriend, the other had moved to a new job elsewhere in London. They were the two with whom he had always sat at coffee breaks, and sometimes had gone to lunch with at a nearby pub. Now there was no one, really, at work, with whom he felt much connection, just people he nodded to at the coffee machine, people he passed in the corridors, he elbowed in the lift.

His parents invited him for Sunday lunch, and he found himself making excuses to get away quickly, to get home for that time between dusk and dark, when curtains remained undrawn. Hurrying down *their* side of the street, he could see before he got there, a dark old upright piano in the front room, the music stand with sheet music spread out. The room was empty, lit like a stage. Waiting. He felt that at any moment someone must come in. He made himself turn away and cross the road and there, outside his house, one of the girls who lived on the ground floor was standing on the front steps, looking blankly at a ripped black sack and the bones of a chicken carcass, which some cat or fox had strewn around. She saw him, said "Bloody mess, isn't it?" and promptly went indoors.

In his own rooms, he looked down. The ruby-red curtains were just being pulled. He could see one hand tugging them across. Upstairs, all was dark. There was a sloping window in the roof, which showed that they had gone into the attics, had built – probably – bedrooms up there. He wondered what they saw of him, if ever they looked up. When he moved in the walls of his room were a pale lime green, which in the summer light had looked fresh; but now he gazed around and thought it just looked cold. And the television cast a chill light, and the bulb in his lamp was too white and strong.

He had a typewriter, an old Adler, bulky and upright. After the flu, he set it up on the table in the window of his living-room, so that he had an excuse to sit in the window and gaze out. If people saw him there they would suppose he was a writer and his idle gaze was in want of inspiration. No one minded if they saw people sitting in their windows at typewriters or drawing boards. But if they saw you just sitting, empty-handed, and staring, people tended to get uncomfortable and wonder what you were up to.

In December his sister invited him to a party. He didn't much want to go, although at one of her parties he had met Harriet, whom he went out with for almost a year. He had been very happy with Harriet, until she met someone she preferred and very gently and tactfully let him down. His mother had liked Harriet too, or she liked the fact that he had, in her words, *found someone* and seemed to be *settling down*. She began to ask tentative questions at those Sunday lunches which almost made him glad when Harriet was gone and he no longer had to put her off with mumbled imprecise replies. He was happy with Harriet, but perhaps he was just happy to have someone to go about with, someone to think of who was thinking of him. The essence of Harriet, what she was really like, stayed rather vague. He went to his sister's party, but not in any mood of hope.

When he got back, the people across the road were having a party of their own. Shapes moved in and out of all the rooms, there was dancing in the room with the piano, and the front door stood open under the redbrick arch as people came and went in the glowing golden hall. The gunning of car engines and the slamming of taxi doors kept him awake long into the night.

There was a hardware shop on a corner in the High Street that had an outdoor section, protected with a high chainlink fence, where in summer they had packs of bedding plants, and bright fuchsias and geraniums in pots. Now, in December, they had Christmas trees stacked there, like corpses in bodybags, lying on their sides in white net tubes. He didn't bother with a tree. Both his parents and his sister would have one in their homes which he could place his presents beneath. But across the road the little girl, the one who seemed too tiny to carry a violin case to school some mornings, was jumping in exasperation on the chequered path, and the boy, bigger, but not much, was swinging on the curly iron gate. He saw them go down the road with their mother in her short, rust-red coat. He saw them come back, in the dusk, the mother and the boy swinging the long corpse of a Christmas tree between them, laughing. The little girl trailed behind, for some reason offended or upset.

The tree appeared in the upstairs room. He went out for a drink with his old friend from work, and when he came back the tree had lights on.

He had come across somewhere the phrase "ami de maison". This he took to mean friend of the household, someone who is friends with each member of a family, not just one in particular, being to each comforter, confessor, court jester, sugar daddy, according to his or her need. He thought that, rather than seeking true love again somewhere, ami de maison would be a marvellous role to fill. He could be the ami de maison to the household across the road. He and they liked the same things, they were musical, they had good taste, they were gregarious, they valued and cherished friendships. He sat behind his Adler with a cup of good coffee and a tiny glass of port, and looked into the glowing Advent calendar window across the road, and wondered how he might introduce himself.

After Christmas, *she* walked down the road in a black coat, long and tight-waisted, and a black Cossack hat. He thought they must be her Christmas presents. Once, she came into the upstairs room in jeans and an old brown jumper, a cup in her left hand, and with her right pulled the thick cream curtains across. But just for a moment before she did so, she paused, gazing out with a dreamy look. She might have been looking right at him. Once *he* walked into the upstairs room, naked to the waist, rubbing his hair vigorously on a blue towel. He was slender, but muscled. Something small and white ran into the room after him, then ran out. Later, it was with them on the way to school: they had got a dog.

The evenings grew lighter, though it was still cold. The blue evening air behind the bare plane tree boughs faded slowly, turning – at what point it was impossible to trace – into thick maroon city night.

He saw her, one day, in her Cossack coat, carrying down the street a tall waving palm, the sort that grows from a coconut-shaped seed only half-submerged in its pot. She was having difficulty in controlling its great long stem. He ran downstairs, hastily inventing an errand to use as an excuse, but by the time he got outside she was at her gate, and opening it, and going in. He had to walk all the way down the road and into Agamemnon Street, and what could he be doing there, where there was nothing but houses, except perhaps calling on a friend? He invented that the friend was out, and walked immediately home.

Afterwards he saw more plants just like it outside the hardware shop. He wondered about buying one for himself.

It came to spring, and in the houses opposite people no longer turned their lights on early. Their curtains remained open, but inside all was dusk. On his side of the road, windows were flung up, and dirty lengths of net curtain trailed out in the breeze. The girls downstairs, once the warm weather arrived, took to dragging old bits of carpet onto the front steps and sitting there, smoking and exposing their white limbs to the air. Upstairs, someone bought a powerful new stereo system.

In May, at eight o'clock one morning, there was a van outside their house. Its ramp was down at the back, and beyond it he could see the open gate, the open front door, the golden hall. Men trailed in and out with boxes. Perhaps the house had become too small, what with the children, and the musical instruments, and now the dog. Perhaps the neighbourhood was getting too shabby, too unsavoury to bring up children in. Perhaps they'd come into money. He had to go to work, but not before he'd seen her, dressed in her jeans and old brown jumper, carry the potted palm out, as if she wanted to oversee it herself into the van. He was there, coming out of his own front door, when she swerved to avoid the removal men with the chaise longue, and he heard the eruption as the pot hit the pavement.

The sun was out when he came home, walking up their side of the road. Someone, perhaps even she, had kicked the shards of broken terracotta into the lee of their front wall, so that no one would step on them. Very quickly, glancing about, he bent and picked up one, a sharp triangular piece, and then crossed the road, and went into his own house.

Smoker

Rachel Cusk

When I saw the article in the newspaper it jumped right out at me and I decided to read it aloud to my "wife" – it was barely six months ago that Lily and I took the plunge, so you'll understand if the word still seems unnatural to me – even though she's said that she's got a "thing" about my reading to her. I like reading things out, little snippets that might make her chuckle or news from abroad she might otherwise miss. Reading aloud was one of the pictures I had in my mind when I thought about Lily and me becoming man and wife. Sometimes, when I do it, she actually gets so "riled" that she puts her hands over her ears. I try shouting, but at times like that I wonder if she even hears what I say.

On this particular occasion, seeing as she was only looking at the TV page, I felt it was safe to proceed.

"Here Lily, listen to this," I declared in a light tone. I have already learned never to let a woman see you're afraid. "Show her the back of your hand now and again," my mother, Margaret, said to me on the eve of our wedding, "and you'll both be better off."

"This'll interest you. 'A man was yesterday found guilty . . .' "

"Gavin, do you mind?" she said, right over me. Her head snapped up and our eyes met. Lily's got lovely eyes, but at that moment I couldn't feel a thing for her.

"It'll only take a minute," I said. " 'A man was yesterday found guilty. . .' "

"For Christ's sake, Gavin! Can't you see I'm reading?"

"I think you're making a mistake," I warned. "I would be prepared to wager that this article will be of interest to you."

Lily didn't reply, just carried on "reading". Looking at her, I had one of those moments I have sometimes had. I've kept these moments a secret from Lily, worried that she might take it the wrong way if I tried to tell her about them. What happens is that suddenly – usually when we've had some tiff or other – I sort of forget who Lily is, in a manner of speaking. That's not the way to put it at all, but words really do escape me when I try to pin this disturbing feeling down. What I mean is that she becomes a stranger to me. She sits there in her sulk, and her body seems to me to fit less and less into our kitchen, not because it gets bigger, you understand, but because it doesn't seem to belong. It's as if a delivery man has come and plonked her in my house, when she was supposed to be taken elsewhere. I sit and stare at her and wonder what she's doing there. Eventually, though, she'll do something characteristic or use a gesture that makes her normal again.

To get on with my story, Lily was "reading", and I was beginning to have one of the moments just described.

"You might even learn something," I continued. "Which is more than can be said for what you're so-called reading."

I thought that was a neat way of putting it, not that I expected any compliments from my "wife". Lily's mouth started to do that thing it sometimes does. She's a very attractive girl, but when her mouth does that you wouldn't look at her twice in the street. The thought has occurred to me that her mouth looks like a rear, if you'll pardon me, when it does that – one of those red rears that monkeys are always waving in your face at the zoo. I haven't told her this. I'm saving it for later, I couldn't say exactly when, but I know that one of these days Lily is going to need a short, sharp shock to wake her up to herself, and I reckon that should do it.

"Oh, for Christ's sake," she said. Her head shot up, but it was only so that she could flick back her hair. Flick! Flick! The way she did it made me think of punching her in the face. Flick! "Just shut up, will you?"

On the eve of our wedding, Lily's father, Derek, told me that if I ever laid a hand on his daughter, he'd "have me". Derek, as you may have guessed, is a thug, but he fancies himself as a bit of a gentleman. Ha, ha! He and his dripping tap of a wife, Pam, live in this "mock" – ha, ha! – Tudor house with a gravel drive which Derek rakes from morning to night. I am always careful to leave a fine pair of skid marks on it when we visit, which isn't often, as you can imagine. The house has three big lights at the front which come on automatically if a "peasant" like me so much as puts his toe past the gate. It makes you feel like a burglar when you come innocently up the drive and those lights go on.

"Your father," I said, continuing my train of thought out loud for Lily's benefit, "has got a lot to answer for. It's him that gave you all these stuck-up ideas about yourself. I don't see it as your fault. But one day you're going to have to wake up to the fact that you're not Derek's little princess any more." I paused. "And that day is going to come soon."

You may think I'm too hard on Lily. Of course, it's impossible for you to imagine what I've been up against since I married her, but as I often say to Margaret when we discuss Lily's problems, it's a tough job and somebody's got to do it. You see, women have changed, and men like me are the ones who pay the price for it. That's what I'm trying to tell you. They don't make them like Margaret any more. Women like Margaret are extinct. These days you pay every penny you've got for them, and then they turn around and say they don't belong to you. Well, they don't actually say it; but a girl like Lily hasn't got her mind on the job and she's happy to let you know it. The more time we spend together, the less I seem to know what's going on in that head of hers. It's not that I don't trust her, don't get me wrong. Lily would never betray me, she knows I'd kill her. It's just that there are things she does, little things, mind, that don't have anything to do with me. Well, you'll say, these days you can't expect a woman to live her life around you. Women want more. That's not the case here. Lily doesn't want anything, I see to that. No, the little things she does that make me suspicious are things which most people probably wouldn't even notice. I notice things, you see. If I enter a room and something's out of place, I notice it, and can't relax until I've set it right. To get back to Lily, I'm not just talking about the silent treatment, although I'd wager you wouldn't find a man who'd put up with that kind of behaviour for as long as I have. Whenever I open my mouth, she acts like I've interrupted something. I'm not saying I'd want a chatterbox around the house, but there's a limit to being quiet, especially when it makes a man feel unwelcome in his own home. But it's not just the silences. It's the whole way she does things. Private, is the only way I can describe the way she does things. It's as if she does things only for herself. I don't want to make out that she's selfish; that would be going too far. The only way I can explain it to you is to say that she does a thing like it was for someone she loved. And that person is her, see? I'm not saying that Lily doesn't love me. Why else would she have married me?

"Not many men would put up with this kind of behaviour," I warned her. "You must think you've got me wrapped around your little finger, just like your fat father was!"

"Put a sock in it, Gav," she said.

She said that, and then she did the thing. She opened her handbag, bold as brass, flicking her hair while she did it. Flick! You may wonder why Lily keeps her bag so close at hand. If she had that bag handcuffed to her wrist she'd forget to carry it about more often.

"What have you got in there," I sometimes say jokingly,

"top secret documents? Has the Prime Minister asked you to keep an eye on something for him, then?"

Why haven't you looked? I hear you ask. She might have drugs in there, or a gun! Lily never lets it out of her sight for a second. I would have to wrestle her to the ground and injure her in some way, which would put me in line for a ticking-off from Derek!

Anyway, as I was saying, right there in the middle of our discussion she opened her precious bag.

"Stop!" I thundered, holding my palm up, like a policeman.

Quick as a flash, she had the packet out.

"Stop now!" I said.

"Give over, Gav," she said, the thing wagging up and down in her mouth. Once she gets it in there, she gets cocky.

"This is your last warning," I said.

I saw that she had the lighter in her hand. When she's got the lighter in her hand and the thing in her mouth, her eyes look as if they're shut. I don't like that look. It's a sex look, if I'm to be frank, and I doubt there's a man alive who'd be happy to see his wife look like that without his help.

I braced myself for the click. I'll be honest with you: there's always a moment, just after the click, when I think her head is going to explode. I don't want it to explode, understand, but at the same time I think it's what she's asking for. Often I hear the explosion, in my own mind, and then the next minute there's smoke everywhere. I see her eyes through it, and that's when I start wishing it really had exploded. It's after that first suck that I hate her the most for the look on her face. She sucks it in and she closes her eyes. She thinks I don't see her, but I do.

"You disgust me," I said.

"Come on, love," she said.

Being called "love" after the first suck means nothing to

me. After the first suck, she's just a slag, and I have no feelings for her.

"Come on," she said again.

Once she's had her fix, then she starts thinking about me. She starts to get a bit worried, sucks up to me a bit. Disgust is the right word to use to describe the way I feel at times like this.

"Leave me alone," I said, coughing.

"Don't start," she said. "Why don't you read me that thing?"

"What thing?" I said, like I'd forgotten.

"In the paper," she said. "Go on, read it."

What gets me when Lily's like this is that she obviously thinks I'm an idiot.

"All right," I said, smiling to make her think I'd forgiven her. I picked up the newspaper and rustled it a bit. "Are you ready?"

The thing was in her mouth again so she just nodded. The flirty way she did it made me sick.

" 'A man was yesterday found guilty,' " I said, quite casually, " 'of manslaughter on the grounds of diminished responsibility after admitting that he was driven to kill his wife by her incessant smoking. Brian Ferret told the court that his wife, Carol, 30, had persistently refused to give up, even after he had threatened to leave her.' "

I looked at Lily, just to see how she was doing. She was listening all right.

" 'Counsel for the defence Richard Bleak told the jury how Ferret, a milkman, had come back from his round to find his wife sitting at the kitchen table smoking. He accused her of having spent the morning smoking while he'd been hard at work. "She was in her own little world," said Mr Bleak. "It was a dark world of dependency, filth and disease. It was a world in which her husband had no place."

'In his anger, Ferret struck his wife over the head with a milk bottle. She lost consciousness and died later in hospital. In his summing up, Justice Thomas Boar advised the jury to show clemency. "Smoking is an evil habit," he said. "Better for a man that his wife betray him with another man than with cigarettes." Sentencing is expected to take place tomorrow.' "

By the time I'd finished, the thing had gone out. Lily just sat there with it between her fingers. I let her sit, reckoning she needed some time to think, while I went about my business.

Hetty Mayvern Decides

Layn Feldman

In February Hetty Mayvern decided that she'd had enough, and that when Pesach came round she wasn't going to eat matzo. Shoin. Over the blessings on the two Seder Nights she could manage, but eight whole days instead of bread? No.

She was sitting on the floor of her kitchen at the time, trying to fix the pipes under her sink. "Why don't they make things properly any more?" she asked the air.

"Bodies aren't built to last," her Manny would say, "why should waste pipes be any different?" Then he'd probably look up from his newspaper and smile at her: "Hey gorgeous, any chance of a cup of tea?"

"It gives me the runs," she told her sister Mona.

"Fine by me," said Mona. "If that's what you want. But speaking for myself, I have to say that if I didn't make my husband matzo bris with the six matzos and four eggs, I might as well say goodbye to my next anniversary present." Why did Mona have to rub salt into the wound? Always. "I would've thought," replied Hetty, "what with his weight problem, not to mention his cholesterol problem, your Barnett could easily go without you making him matzo bris ever again." And just in case Mona had a good comeback, Hetty quickly replaced the receiver and phoned her friend Kitty.

"Have you been to the doctor's?" asked Kitty.

"No."

"Do you have a raging thirst that cannot be quenched?"

"No, why?"

"Have you lost a lot of weight recently?"

"Kitty. Remember when we were little and Tessy Rabin got the measles and you played with her and then you got the measles?"

"So?"

"So just because your son's got a medical degree, doesn't mean you're going to get it."

"I was only just asking," said Kitty, "because Milly Popoff had the runs with matzo after she found out she was diabetic."

"I'm not diabetic."

"Then if you've never had trouble before I don't think I can help you."

What went wrong? The conversation had started out on the right track, but then somewhere along the way, Kitty had suddenly taken a left turn when she should've gone straight on. Same sort of thing would happen when she and Manny used to sit in their car on a Sunday, and Hetty would say, "Let's go and see someone nice for a change." Manny would say, "Okay," and then drive off to his brother's house.

A lightbulb in the hall needed changing so Hetty got out the tall ladder. If she was diabetic, God forbid, at least that would make her decision easier. Her God understood that if you had to take medicine during Yom Kippur, then you had to take it to be well over the fast. But how far would understanding go, even with a letter from your doctor?

"Maybe if you're worried you could try an experiment," suggested her daughter Jackie. "You could take one of those diarrhoea tablets beforehand and then eat some matzo. See what happens."

"And then I could eat some bread?"

"No Mum. You have to have exactly the same conditions as there would be if it were Pesach, otherwise you can't see if it works."

"Why did you have to become a Science teacher?" her

mother asked, "why couldn't you do something else like drive a cab?"

"Then I'd be even more argumentative."

"Not possible."

"So you gonna do it?"

"No."

"Why not?"

"Because in order to get into the mood I feel ill already, so it makes no sense when I try hard not to get ill, to get ill just to try it. I know what being ill feels like. What's more I don't think the J.C. has passed those tablets as kosher for Pesach."

"Ah. So when Moses came down from Mount Sinai with the Ten Commandments, the real reason he broke them was because the *Jewish Chronicle* hadn't passed those particular tablets as kosher for Pesach. Mum, I'm sure your God wouldn't mind if you didn't eat matzo."

"Even so," sighed Hetty, "I don't like to disappoint people."

In March they began to stock boxes of matzos in the supermarkets. "Buy Two Get One Free" ran the advert. Hetty stood before the pyramid of cartons waiting for a sign. To buy or not to buy. Nothing happened, so she turned towards the bread aisle. What am I going to do, she thought, if during Pesach I run out of bread and have to go buy a loaf? Only thing was, that year Passover was going to fall exactly the same time as Easter. Hetty froze to the spot as she considered the terrifying thought: In the whole of Golders Green – nothing will be open! She took a few tentative steps.

Could I buy lots of bread beforehand, Hetty wondered, and freeze it? Would her God mind if she froze a cholla, a coupla platzels? Or would that be in bad taste? Would a bulka be worse than a large sliced Hovis?

A man about Hetty's age was standing staring at the bread. "Twenty-seven varieties," he said, "I counted them. So I ask you: what does a man do when his doctor tells him to eat more brown bread because of the fibre, but it doesn't toast anything like a white? You woulda thought by now that someone would've come up with the idea of making a small loaf that was half brown and half white. For the aesthetics they could have a sliced loaf that alternated: white brown white brown. And to demonstrate that we live in an egalitarian society, you could have the same number of loaves that went brown white brown white . . ."

Hetty remembered a cousin who talked like this. "What about buying a small brown and a small white?"

The man turned to study Hetty's face. "That would be the logical answer," he said, "but it would be a waste for me on my own now."

"How do you get on with matzo?" Hetty ventured (boldly she thought afterwards).

The man seemed to brighten up. "Now there's a completely different animal. D'you know, one year I had the most terrible trouble with matzo. To me it tasted like cardboard. This was only during Pesach mind you. I thought: Why should this be like it is? Then I thought: on all other days matzo tastes wonderful with a little chopped liver, dipped in chicken soup or lightly buttered. So why on these days – meaning the whole of Pesach, the days as well as the nights – it should taste like cardboard? Eventually I came to this conclusion: eight days out of three hundred and sixty-five isn't such a bad deal. I had a look at it with the new calculator my son brought over from Canada. It works out as roughly 2 per cent. So I reckon if the Israelites can put up with having to serve all those years with rigour, I can put up with a little hardship, a little discomfort for 2 per cent of the time." He now seemed breathless from talking. "I think that's the most I've spoken to any one person in a very long time."

Hetty glanced down at his shoes. They were brightly polished. She wanted to ask him if he'd been in the Army during the War. "Were you in Italy or North Africa at all? Did you ever by chance come across a Private Manny

Mayvern?" She was on the point of asking, but then the moment passed.

"Strictly speaking," continued the stranger, "unleavened bread is unleavened bread, whether it's a cream cracker or a cheese straw. I mean it simply is bread, biscuits etc, made from a dough containing no yeast or leavening."

Hetty didn't know how to answer, so she offered: "My daughter says there's a lot of fibre in dried fruit and fresh fruit and veg."

"I know," the man said, "but toasted swede with marmalade and butter doesn't quite hit the spot."

They stood in companionable silence, both trying to remember when life wasn't so complicated; then the man reached out, took a crusty white from the shelves, and waved a goodbye.

As the first Seder night approached, Golders Green began to fill up with tourists. Hetty went to buy some fuse wire. "They drive up in their big fancy cars," complained Mr Hennytink the shopkeeper, "they don't know how to double park properly, they spend a fortune in all the food shops, and then they rush home with the fruits of their pillaging."

"Business not so good, Mr Hennytink?" Hetty asked.

"Terrible," he replied.

Jackie phoned. "My upstairs neighbour Mrs Uppeldown – I told you about her – is ill. So I went in to see if there was anything she wanted from the shops . . ."

"Don't tell me. She asked you to buy some traif."

"Worse."

"She wants you to carry the pig home on your head."

"She wants me to go and pick up her newspaper tomorrow."

"Ah, that Mrs Uppeldown. Couldn't you ask for a brown paper bag?"

"Mum. When did you last see a brown paper bag?"

"Buy a magazine and roll it up inside."

"No. Either I go in there and buy it or I don't."

"Why can't you just say you're picking it up for a neighbour?"

"For the simple reason no one, nobody, is actually going to stand there and question me about it. I wouldn't mind at all if Henry Goldbloom turned and said, 'Oh Jackie, not able to read words of more than one syllable any more?' But he won't. I'd just get a look. And if I answer that look it means I'm on the defensive, which means I feel guilty."

"So what you gonna do?"

"I'm going to go in there and ask Mrs Patel if she could have the newspaper delivered to Mrs Uppeldown." Hetty could imagine looking across at Manny and him smiling back at her. "The girl must've got the brains from somewhere."

Two days later Hetty decided to start her spring cleaning. She put on her heavy-duty housework clothes – a huge white jumper that had been Jackie's first attempt at knitting, and a pair of bright orange ski pants, her daughter-in-law's first attempt at being trendy. Manny always said Hetty looked like a piece of gefilte fish.

"What about the orange slacks?"

"Okay. Gefilte fish garnished with carrot."

Hetty wished she could be more like her sister Greta, who had different sets of rubber gloves for different jobs around the house. Pink mediums were for washing up, thin blue for dusting, and double strength bright yellow ones for the ugly jobs. "Listen," said Greta, "if I can clean a baby's tush, in fact three tushes, six if you want to count grandchildren so far – then I can tackle anything."

"But what about the things Joe used to do?"

"My eldest son comes over to fix all the electrical stuff, my middle son comes over to deal with the plumbing and heating, and my youngest son comes over to eat me out of house and home. So where you going for the Seder Nights?"

"Jackie's making the first, which means it'll be my very first vegetarian Passover meal, with all the story read out aloud, including the commentary . . ."

"... And it'll be an hour and a half before you get to eat..."

"With no noshing in between, not even an olive... Then Dovi's making the second night and insisted (yet again) on doing all the cooking. To compensate we'll probably race through the story to get to the meal."

"At least you'll see your grandchildren."

"Who knows. Maybe this year it'll be cool to be seen talking to your Booba."

As April and the forthcoming Pesach got closer, Hetty found more repair work that needed doing round the house. She rang her son Dovi, the counsellor.

"Mum, I think you may need to take on board the idea that you may possibly be trying to avoid tackling a difficult issue here."

"You mean like when my Sunday newspaper can't get through the letterbox?"

"Dad died around this time of year didn't he?"

"You asking or telling me?"

"Maybe Pesach, or rather the advent of Pesach, stirs up some pretty sad memories that you want to run away from."

"Sad memories make me cry, they don't give me diarrhoea."

"I still see a connection here. Could be that you're holding onto something when really you could, perhaps should let go of it. Maybe it's the lingering in the last stages of bereavement, a sort of transitional phase, can take years to get through..."

"If you say so."

"Let go and you'll grow, believe me, Mum."

"I've done all the growing I need to do." Hetty tried to calm herself. She loved her son, but he didn't talk the same any more. It was as though everything he wanted to say had to go through some sort of process before it reached her. Food passed as Kosher for Passover, thoughts passed as Kosher for Counselling? "Dovi," she asked kindly, "do you still want me to hold onto that fort you made; the wooden one with all spikes round it?"

"You mean the one I made in Mr Carter's class?"

"I'm having a clear-out of rubbish . . ."

"That's not rubbish!"

". . . And it's just sitting on top of a wardrobe gathering dust . . . So what I'm asking is do you want me to keep it? Shall I throw it away, or will you take it home? Please." Hetty waited.

"That's an important part of my childhood. You can't throw that away."

Her son sounded hurt so Hetty left it at that. "I'll hold onto it then, yes?" she said softly. "For the time being."

At the end of March Hetty spoke to her grandson Elliott.

"Booba," he said, "I was looking through the Haggadah you bought me."

"The book with the tabs to pull to make things happen?"

"Yeah."

"I'm glad you liked it. Have you drowned Pharaoh's army yet?"

"My friend Lawrence has one where Moses' staff turns into a snake."

"How does that work?"

"He's got a special computer program . . . Mum says I have to ask the four kashas this year . . ."

"So I've heard. It's a great honour, means you're not a baby any more."

"Booba please. It's just another excuse for grownups to get you to do things you don't want to do."

"Tattala, did you ring me to moan because your mother has asked you to clear up your bedroom, or is there some other reason for this phone call?"

"You know where Dad picks up the matzo and says:" (Elliott put on his reading-out-aloud voice) "This matzo or unleavened bread that we eat – what is the reason for it? It is because at the time when God appeared in His glory to rescue our forefathers from Egypt, they had to leave hastily and they took with them their unleavened dough." (His voice returned to normal.) "So the man you met in the supermarket was wrong. Because Booba, my teacher says that it was going to be proper bread, but the Israelites didn't have time to wait for the dough to rise. Does that help you?"

"No my shayn kint, it makes me feel more confused, but thank you for taking the time and trouble."

"So that means I'm not the dull son, am I?"

"No, why?"

"And I can't be the one that hasn't the wit to ask, or the wicked son, can I Booba?"

"No."

"Which means I must be the wise son."

"Yes Elly, you must be the wise son."

"Thank you, he said politely. Then he roared out to his sister: "LEAH! BOOBA JUST SAID I MUST BE THE WISE SON, WHICH MEANS YOU MUST BE THE IDIOT IN THIS FAMILY!"

A few days before Pesach Hetty lit a Yatzheit for Manny. "These days," said Mr Hennytink, "most people are buying the electric candle. You just plug it in and switch it on for when you want it. So much safer they say, nu?" He looked at Hetty, wanting her to be as delighted with his new toy as he obviously was.

"Would you use one?" she asked.

He peered at her over his glasses. "Are you kidding?" So Hetty decided on an old-fashioned do-it-yourself flame, and the next day she went to the estate agents and put her house on the market.

She still suffered with matzo that year, but when she eventually went to the doctor he told her to add more fibre to her diet. Perhaps, thought Hetty, she could find someone to share the expense of a small white loaf and a small brown one when Pesach came round again.

Moving Back

Cathy Cullis

Nancine shows me the sampler she has stitched for her home. Brown thread on coffee-coloured linen to make it look old. It says:

I care not who you serve,
but in this house
we serve God.

It is in a smart frame. I want to say, if I stitched that I would make it funny, something like "I care not who you serve, as long as it's me first," but before I get the chance, Nancine has hooked the sampler back on the hallway wall and has walked further into the house to instruct her daughter, Monique, to put the parakeet in its cage and pour us all a soda.

I hate birds and am grateful to Nancine for remembering this, since we have not seen each other for two years. She would not appreciate a grown woman peeing herself on the sofa because a small, greyish-white bird is screeching, "Get me Cheerios" from the light fitting above.

Nancine and I used to work together at Modern Woman at the Paradise Valley shopping mall. Then I got bored and somehow persuaded my husband to leave Phoenix to visit my home country, England. I had left there aged fourteen and had only been back twice in ten years. Simon got a job with his banking company in London and managed to stick it out for a whole twenty-three months and three weeks . . .

Three sodas later David arrives home, sweaty and gritty from riding his precious Harley all the way down Camelback in the rush-hour. He stands in the doorway and straightens his bandanna, just looking over at Nancine and me pretending to chat. David is Nancine's nephew, although there are fewer than ten years between them. He came from Indiana to sleep on her sofa for two weeks, three years ago.

I watch him and it excites me just a little to notice he has not changed in two years. The same hand on hip as he opens the fridge door. The exact same sniff before taking a swig from his bottle of beer. Eventually he says hi from a distant corner of the open-plan kitchen and asks if it's been cool in England or "just fucking freezing." He asks if I'm glad to be back and I shrug in agreement. England is home but yes, it is cold and hubby got rusty with all that rain. Then he asks Nancine's permission to watch television and permission granted he struts into the adjoining family room and throws himself boots-and-all on the couch.

David watches a religious channel. "Send me your tithe," the televisual preacher is squealing. I look into the family room from where I am seated, expecting to see David sneering with tongue partially hanging – a facial expression of his I remember well – but instead he is cross-legged and thoughtfully frowning like a young boy listening to his grandmother talk about life before VCRs. "Can I check out your Bible, Nancine?" he yells and she replies, "Sure, bedroom counter," and he says, "Hebrews something" and flies into her downstairs room for the book.

I glance over at Nancine hoping for an explanation. Since when has David been interested in Bible stuff?

Nancine gets up and invites me into her yard to see how well her orange and grapefruit trees are doing. It is January but in the Arizona desert all things "summery" bloom at this time of year. Filling the rest of the yard is what looks like an Olympic-sized trampoline.

"Oh, this guy I've been dating bought it for Monique to

keep fit as there's so much sugar in all this fat-free stuff we eat . . ." Nancine looks down at the dusty lawn and adjusts her spectacles. "Don't think there's anything . . . it's not like we sleep together or . . . We met at church. Since the new pastor and the idea to wear name tags it's been a whole lot easier to get to know people . . ." She lifts up her head and giggles but looks away and quickly pulls an orange from a tree, and hands it to me. "Here," she says, rubbing the fruit into my hand, "they're good ones, believe me."

We drive to the grocery store, off Thunderbird, for meat and salad supplies. Nancine has decided to cook a barbecue for us all, plus the new mystery man in her life, who is due to show up after work and a game of pool at Hooters.

Nancine parks up in a "carts only" space and we walk into the store. Monique complains she is thirsty and asks to be allowed to sit in the coffee shop and have a Pepsi, but her request is denied. Near to tears, she walks ahead of us with the trolley, slamming it into special offer stands, filing it with pretzels, soda, Ben and Jerry's ice-cream and teen deodorant.

"I keep hoping she'll calm after a time," Nancine confesses to me in the kitchen paper aisle – we have lost Monique. "The divorce was six years ago but . . . I guess you don't have to worry like this, having no kids. I told Samuel – that's the guy I'm seeing by the way – I told Samuel that Paula has decided no kids for a time and I guess she has a sensible perspective . . . He's a neat kinda guy. Respectful, I think. Well, he's the first guy I've dated in a long while. It feels good . . ."

Eventually, we find Monique in the magazine section, flipping through a copy of *New Woman*. She looks up and too hastily stuffs the magazine back into the rack. It rips. She turns a speckled scarlet. *New Woman* is forbidden territory as yet, I suppose. Nancine sighs and takes the trolley, and wheels it calmly to an available check-out.

Monique shows up again only after all the groceries are packed. She purchases a tube of Lifesavers with her own money and leads us out the store.

David is sat on a stool in the kitchen, facing the wall. He is on the telephone. He whispers but I can hear the name Lisa repeated over. I smile at him as I help Nancine unpack the groceries. It is highly unlikely that we will have a barbecue, considering the purchases made, but Nancine has said nothing. Monique is cooing to the parakeet in its cage and begging it sweetly to say "pretty one," or at least hello. She seems a little less maudlin.

David hangs up the telephone and twists about on his stool to face us. "So, what's cooking?" he asks before seeing the bags of chips, pretzels, cookies . . .

"Oh Monique's decided to treat us all," Nancine declares, opening the freezer to put away the three tubs of ice-cream, "we're ordering pizza."

We sit in the yard, just David and me, chewing on giant slices of soggy pizza delivered only minutes ago but already cold. It is getting dark but there are no stars, only the distant light of an aircraft marks the sky. Now we are out of the house, Nancine and Monique are yelling at each other, but we make no comment. I wonder what time Samuel is expected but before I have a chance to ask David if he knows, he throws his pizza onto the lawn and rests his hand on my shoulder.

"Paula, I'm so glad we've gotten – I mean I've gotten this opportunity to speak . . ." This is not David talking. What's he playing at, I wonder? "I need to ask you for something," he says. "I wish to ask your forgiveness."

I stop eating and stare into the lights of the house. I can see the rooms are empty; Nancine and Monique must have moved their fight upstairs.

"It's something I need to do, since I am now a Christian. Well, it's part of my initiation, if you will – into the heart of the Lord." David looks at me with serious, sparkling eyes. He still has that more-than-rough-around-the-edges look about him. When I knew him before the only time he mentioned the "Lord" word was to say something like, "Lord I could shit all day and not feel bruised . . ."

"I need your forgiveness for what happened between us – the fornicating stuff," David insists. He wipes his nose on the back of his hand and shrugs. "Shit, you know what I mean, Paula. I'm only asking for a simple little forgive you." I feel myself blushing but I don't know why. What did we do together that was so bad? "Oh hell Paula, God forgive me, you know, the times in the pool back at the apartments – don't you remember?"

I stare down at his scuffed black leather biker boots. They must be the same boots he was wearing two years ago. Either that or he can scuff boots in the exact same way. I remember those boots very clearly. I remember staring at them sitting by the pool as we swam together. I remember looking up at them as I waited for him to "surprise me" by quietly swimming up behind me and pulling my leg. . . .

"That time I grabbed your tittie . . ." He looks away from me, as if with shame, yet I know he feels none. How can he? And why use that pathetic word – tittie. He never used that word before. "That was just the beginning of trouble," he confesses. "Please forgive me for not respecting you, your body, your wisdom as a woman – and a married woman."

"Why?" I say. "Why?" I ask again. "Nancine asked you to either become a Christian or leave her house," I suggest.

David stares at me, or rather over my left shoulder. He sucks in his cheeks. Now he looks like he's been smoking dope. I recognise the expression well. "She asked me to consider the guidance of God – I mean that with the guidance of God I could become a better person, and I have . . ."

"I can't forgive you, David. You – we – didn't do anything wrong," I say.

"But you must – "

"No David, I shan't."

David scowls. Although it is quite dark now I can see his joined brows, his drooping mouth. I sit up in my seat. I am being strong, sticking to my principles. He does not think I have any, but I do.

"But I touched you – a married lady, Paula," David insists.

"So, you grabbed my breast – once."

"It was twice. And we kissed – underwater."

"What difference does underwater make? We were playing shark. Being kids again."

"I just wanted to . . ."

"What? If I remember things the right way you had plenty of girlfriends. Are you asking all of them to forgive you? You must have done far worse with some of them . . ."

"It was different with you, Paula. You were a married woman. And I liked you. So just forgive me. Just say, I forgive you, even if it doesn't mean much to you."

"I'm sorry, I can't."

The patio area is suddenly lit by a bluish, lilac light. I turn to see a tall, lean, well-tanned guy in tight jeans.

He walks closer to us. "What is this with you guys sitting in the dark out here, huh?"

"Hey Samuel, what's up?" David replies, quickly getting up from his yard seat. Samuel smacks him on the back and David makes a strange little squeaking sound.

"So, you must be Paula from England. How was it over there – foggy?" Samuel says, holding his hand out to me.

I shake Samuel's hand and decide to play along. "Oh yes, as always, it's always foggy back home."

Samuel knocks back his head and laughs. His laugh is almost silent, coming from the pit of his stomach, it seems. I notice he is wearing a small gold cross in one ear that does not quite suit him. It looks a little effeminate somehow. He turns away and walks back into the house with David quickly following behind, so I too follow.

Nancine is busy in the kitchen, bashing two frozen steaks with a mallet. She hits the icy meat with all her might, it appears, but all the time she is grinning, or maybe just gritting her teeth. I look about for David but he has disappeared.

"Samuel must have his meat," Nancine explains, between blows. "Only some of us can live on soda and potato chips." She glances over at Monique, who is sat on the sofa with her school books spread about. Her face is blotchy from crying and every so often she pronounces a sniff.

"Hey, what's with you Monique, my little sugar?" Samuel says, budging her along the sofa with his tiny ass, so he can sit next to her. Her school books spill onto the floor, but neither she or he pick them up. "What's with all this work, huh? Now why don't you go outside and have a good bounce on that tramp, work off some of those candy calories, huh?"

"I'm not feeling like bouncing," Monique protests, only slightly grumpy. She puts down her fountain pen and uses the tips of her fingers to tidy her sun-bleached hair. "Maybe later Samuel, okay?" The smile that follows this is just a little nervous.

"I hear you did good and bounced a whole hour just after school today, so that's okay," Samuel then says, squeezing her knee.

David and Samuel are talking God, in the family room. They swig from beer bottles. Samuel likes to talk loudly with the help of strong hand motions. David does not say all that much, just sits there with one hand scratching away at his chin. He must really mean it, I think. He must really want to go through with it. Why else would David be sitting here taking all this from Samuel?

Nancine calls me back into the kitchen. I have been spying and she gives me that knowing look, like the time I peeped into a cubicle at Modern Woman to see what a size twenty-eight really looks like. She says she has made coffee for us. I would actually prefer a beer but I say nothing. Monique has her arms wrapped around her mother's waist. She is begging to brush Nancine's long hair. After a little half-hearted shrugging-off and moaning, Nancine agrees. Monique rushes to her room to fetch her brushes and a mirror.

Monique gets Nancine to kneel up on the carpet. I smile at them and Nancine smiles at me. Whilst Monique combs out tiny knots and bites off split ends, we chat about the old days when we worked together. We talk about the time Mrs Brieheart, the manageress at Modern Woman – the store for the larger lady – tried to put us both on a high-fat diet to make us more presentable to customers.

I really want to discuss David and his conversion toward the light of God, but again this is not the appropriate time – until Monique goes to her room to fetch bands and grippers.

"I just want to ask you quickly," I half-whisper, in case the guys can hear from the family room. "Can you tell me what's going on with David?"

"What's going on with him?" Nancine replies, wrinkling her nose. "Oh, you mean becoming a Christian?"

"Yes. Why? I mean, did you persuade him?"

"There's no need to whisper," Nancine replies in a loud voice. "We're all pleased David goes to church these days. I'm very happy for him. You should come along now you're back in town – if you feel able to, that is." Nancine looks around her and leans toward me. She whispers. "The half-truth of it is, Paula, and I'm not really to say this, God forgive me, but the thing is Samuel has gotten David a j-o-b." I frown at her. "It's not a temporary contract thing, either," Nancine continues. "Samuel is a builder, see, and now David is in training. They're constructing new homes on Indian School . . ."

"Why could you not tell me this before, Nancine?" I ask.

"Because. Because David asked me not to."

Nancine has at least fifteen bands in her hair. She looks like a Rastafarian. Or a Medusa. Monique lies on the carpet beside her mother, giggling frantically.

"What have you done to me?" Nancine says, holding a mirror up to look. "If Samuel comes in here right now . . ." But she cannot help giggling herself.

David comes into the room. He asks to speak with me alone. Nancine does not look at either of us. Monique is now writhing hysterically.

Samuel comes into the room. He sees Nancine and sneers at her. He grips Monique by the arm and pulls her up from the floor. He suggests she goes into the yard to bounce for a while. She looks at him fearfully with tears down her cheeks. Her lips quiver. She goes out into the yard. Nancine begins to pull the bands out of her hair.

I follow David out of the room, but Samuel stops us. "Hey, have you seen Nancine's bird? He's a cute one."

"Yes. He's very pretty but I don't actually like birds," I reply.

"You don't actually like birds?" Samuel queries. "A bird is a bird. What's it gonna do to you, huh? Bite ya!"

"I just don't like them," I say, sitting back down by Nancine.

David stands twitching, as if he wants to say something. "I can vouch for her fear," David announces suddenly. It is as if he is declaring a sin.

"Birds are important creatures," Samuel says, "if you've read your Bible you'll know that. It was a dove who helped man overcome the flood. Let's see if we cannot help you overcome this thing," he suggests, strutting over to the bird cage. The bird appears to be asleep.

"I would really rather not," I say.

Nancine is now quickly brushing her hair. She looks up at me and we exchange worried glances. Somehow I know she will not say anything to stop Samuel. It will be up to me to stand up to him.

Samuel walks over to me, with the bird in the cage. The bird still appears to be sleeping. I think about getting up from the sofa. Maybe I will just make a slightly cowardly excuse like going to see how Monique is doing in the yard. Then I think perhaps Monique is best left alone. I imagine Samuel following me out into the yard and standing by the trampoline, counting Monique's jumps.

Samuel sits the bird cage down on the coffee table nearby. He kneels down and gets ready to open the cage. He turns his head and smiles at me. It is not a devilish smile. I think, in his heart he really does think he can work a miracle here.

I look up to see David watching from a little distance, with arms folded. He appears to have stopped twitching but looks suddenly very sweaty.

"Are we ready for this?" Samuel says, finger still on the cage catch. "Don't worry, I know how to handle him. He's a beautifully tamed creature. You have nothing to fear whatsoever."

"Samuel, I appreciate your interest in my – "

But it is too late. The door is open and the bird is free. It flaps and flies. I close my eyes and try to think of anything other than that bird flying at me, the wings fluttering in my hair . . .

"Come on now Tweetie Pie, get on my wrist you flirty bird," Samuel says in a high-pitched voice.

I bury my head in my lap. I don't care if I am labelled a coward. My hands cover my head and hair completely – just don't let it near me . . .

"Come on Tweetie, you flirty bird, get on my wrist now," Samuel demands.

I raise my head just a little, just enough so that I can see what is going on. Out of the corner of my eye I see David holding the bird on his arm and stroking it. Thinking of touching the filthy creature makes me nauseous. I bury my head in my lap, although I think with David holding the bird I am quite safe.

"Hey buster, what's wrong with Samuel's arm, huh?" Samuel says. "What's the problem David, hand him over."

"No," I hear David say.

There is a moment's silence. Then Nancine requests the bird be placed back in its cage.

More silence. I look up. David is still holding the bird. He is stroking the bird but there is no affection in his actions. He appears to be trembling and is still sweating.

"What is this?" Samuel says.

Then Monique comes in from the yard and the bird flies out.

David stands on the trampoline, holding an electric lantern. He has stopped looking about the yard and is now just up there, staring into the dark.

"It'll make its way home, sure enough," Nancine says, although she does not sound so certain. "This isn't the first time it's just flown out like that."

Samuel has gone home, so Monique has come out of her room to help look for the bird. Even I have been looking for the bird. Nancine told me to stay inside and watch television, but for some reason I do not mind the idea of looking, or even finding the creature.

David turns round and shines the lantern at me. The light hits me between the eyes. "What?" I say, but he does not speak.

Nancine looks at me quickly and then looks away. She walks over to a grapefruit tree and half-heartedly searches through the branches. Monique goes into the house.

David switches the lantern off and jumps down from the trampoline. He walks over to me and offers his hand. We shake. I feel his sweaty palm in my hand and I do not want to let it go. I am scared for him.

"Do you see what I see?" Nancine says. She is staring

up at something. "The bastard was up there all the time, God forgive me."

I look up to see what looks like the parakeet perched on the tip of the porch roof. It looks down at us with indifference, or at least I imagine it is indifferent, if birds can be like that.

"You want to know something, you guys?" Nancine says. "I never have honestly cared for that thing. I mean, it can be cute alright. If it's in a good mood. Yeah, if it's in a good mood it'll tweet until you're sick of hearing it. But most of the time all I can think about is how much that cage stinks."

"Are you suggesting what I think you're suggesting?" David then says.

"What do you reckon on survival rate?" Nancine asks.

"I'd say pretty good," David reassures her. "He'll find someone else to pester soon enough, you can be sure of that, I suppose."

"What do you think, Paula?" Nancine asks me.

"I prefer to see birds high up, Nancine," I say. "Maybe he'll just roost there for a time, if that's what parakeets do?"

"Lord, I don't know what parakeets are supposed to do," Nancine says. "It's getting cold out here, let's go inside and see if that little missy of mine has used her good brain and made us some hot chocolate."

How Are You?

Deborah Moggach

Her husband used to say: "I never knew we had so many friends until we built the swimming pool."

It was true. The moment the sun came out the phone used to ring. "Diana, how are you?" people would say. "How's Malcolm? Haven't seen you for ages."

"Come round for tea," she would reply, "for drinks. Have a swim."

"A swim?" They would sound surprised, as if this was the last thing on their minds. "What a wonderful idea."

She had liked it, actually – summer arriving, swallows arriving, her neighbours arriving with their costumes already on under their clothes. That was what the pool was for – that and Malcolm's heart. Their doctor had recommended swimming – cardiovascular exercise – and Malcolm, who had just retired, said: "I've always wanted a pool. Better late than never."

When people rang now, they said: "Diana, how are you?" Their tone was different. "How *are* you, Di?"

Eight months had passed and the phone calls were less frequent but the tone was always there. She heard it in the village, in the post office, in Sainsbury's. They would break off their conversations and turn to her. "Di?" Their voices low and sympathetic. "How *are* you?" When she left there was a respectful pause; then, when she was nearly out of earshot, their conversation would resume – low at first and then gathering normality like a train gathering speed.

It was June – the first hot week of summer. Nobody had phoned yet, inviting themselves obliquely over for a swim. Maybe the idea of splashing about in a pool seemed too trivial for a house of grief, maybe they didn't want to intrude. They didn't understand that it made no difference; she felt just the same, surrounded by other people. Nothing made any difference. It just seemed a waste; she had had the man around to clean the pool and check the filter, whatever men did. When he left she took off her clothes and sank into the water. It closed over her head, warm as tears.

Her most regular visitor was her daughter Meredith. In the early weeks Meredith had come to stay a great deal, to keep her company, but to tell the truth her presence had been a mixed blessing. Her daughter's bullying protectiveness was so tiring.

"Don't see anyone you don't want to see! Why should you go to the Taylors for drinks?"

"I don't mind," said Diana, "they're just being kind."

"They're so ghastly. Such ghastly Tories."

"Even Tories can be kind."

Meredith would try to rally her, dragging her round the house. "Let's wash these sofa covers, they're filthy, where's the zip?"

Sometimes Diana felt like a patient who had taken an overdose; her daughter was the nurse, marching her up and down and slapping her cheeks to keep her from sliding into unconsciousness. Meredith, never the most intuitive of women, didn't understand that most things were simply beyond Diana's reach – literally so, sometimes, when she couldn't get things from the top shelf. Malcolm had put them there, Malcolm knew how to do it. And then there was everything else – the screwtops she couldn't unscrew, the rusted lightbulbs she couldn't replace. Everything.

"He kept you in a doll's house. It's like Ibsen," said

Meredith, who taught Communication Studies. "He kept you from learning how to cope."

"I didn't want to learn," said Diana. "He did it."

Her daughter just snorted. Diana couldn't tell her the truth – that even after eight months, when she should be getting better, it was such an effort to do anything at all. On the bad days she had to concentrate through each moment, just to get to the end of them. The nearest sensation was the pain of childbirth; the way you couldn't be distracted. And then there were the little things which suddenly walloped her, as if she had been hit with a sock full of sand. When her son, for instance, had helped her sell Malcolm's Rover and she saw the tax disc so confidently paid up until May. He had presumed he would live that long; don't we all?

But her son had long since returned to Zurich – he was a banker – and that just left Meredith. She had had a difficult relationship with her father and his desertion, through dying, seemed to inflame her rage against men in general as well as him in particular. When she was little her nickname had been "Merry" but it was hard to imagine anyone calling her that now. She had grown into a big, troubled adult and soon after the birth of her son, Zak, she had become a lesbian. Recently she had ballooned in girth. In Diana's head her husband said: "Why do all lesbians get fat? Or should I say adiposally challenged?"

Meredith and Zak arrived on Saturday morning. "How are you?" asked Meredith, dumping down her stuff in the hall.

Diana said: "I was thinking yesterday, people ask me this but with this peculiar emphasis. How *are* you. Before your father died they'd say how are *you*? What's significant about this? In the old days they were interested in me, and now they're interested in the process, the *areness* of it? You should know, you teach Communication Studies."

Meredith sniffed. "The house smells funny. We must find you another cleaning lady."

"You haven't answered my question."

"It's a denial of communication."

"What – not answering my question?"

"No – what they're doing. They just want you to say *I'm fine*." Her square face, framed by shorn hair, looked at her mother. "You're not eating properly. You look thin."

"I'm fine," said Diana.

They went out into the garden. Meredith looked at the vegetable patch. "I'd better get cracking on that," she said.

"Somebody's given me some runner bean plants. I've been meaning to put them in." Diana thought: one day, surely, I'll feel hungry enough to want to eat beans again. Surely, by the time they are ripe.

The poles still stood, from last year. Last year's withered plants, beige tatters, still clung to them. Malcolm had tied the strings and she hadn't been able to bring herself to untie the knots his fingers had worked on. No wonder she never got anything done.

"We can dig a new bed for them over there," said Meredith.

"That's where Norman's buried!" cried Zak. Norman, their dog, had got run over two years ago. "Will he be a skeleton by now?" asked Zak.

"Go off and play!" said his mother.

Zak picked up a worm. "Wonder how many worms it took to eat him."

"Zak!" said his mother.

"It's all right," said Diana. It was true. She only minded things when another person was there; to mind on their behalf was so tiring.

Zak, slashing at nettles, wandered off. He was nine. For Malcolm, Zak had stopped at eight and a bit. Malcolm knew nothing of his grandson's new compulsion to buy lottery scratch-cards; the new mannerism he had, of rubbing his nose and saying "wicked'. This made Diana feel strange, but it had its advantages. On his last visit Zak had bragged about how some boys in his class had been caught glue-sniffing and Diana had felt an unexpected jolt of relief, that her husband had been spared being upset by this. He had been spared eight months' toll of terrible newspaper stories. He had died, innocent of the knowledge of the Oklahoma bombing. He need no longer worry about how Zak was to grow up in a lesbian household without a father of his own. Wasn't that something?

"Don't do that," said Diana to her daughter. "Come and have a swim. Enjoy yourself." She nearly added: enjoy yourself, because you don't know how long you've got.

Meredith didn't swim, however. She sat beside the pool reading a book called *You Don't Listen: Men and Women Talking*. She had put on even more weight. Zak jumped in and splashed around. "There's lots of dead things in here," he called. "Some of them aren't quite dead." He rose up from the shallow end, a struggling insect on his finger.

"See how many you can rescue!" called Diana.

Meredith, who was a vegetarian, said: "He's always killing things. I try to tell him it's wrong, it's all bloody testosterone."

"He's a bit young for that."

"No male is too young for that."

"So you want him to be a New Man," said Diana. A wave of loneliness hit her. She thought: I don't want a new man. I want the old one back. To hide her face, she went back to the house to fetch some drinks.

She went into the kitchen. Sometimes she felt as if she were underwater, so slowly did she move; it was like pushing against the current. She poured out some wine for herself and some orange juice for her daughter and grandson. The fact that Meredith didn't drink suddenly irritated her. Her daughter was training to be a counsellor but Diana thought that she would do a lot more good if they could simply crack open the gin bottle and get sloshed together.

She opened the ice-making compartment. The door fell off, clattering onto the floor. "Blast!" It always did this. Only Malcolm knew how to wedge it closed on its stupid plastic hinge. "Time for a snort," he'd say, looking at his watch. "Gin and tonic, old fruit?" He'd yank open the ice-making compartment, push out some cubes and shove it back, kicking it with his foot. Sometimes he didn't refill the tray with water; it used to drive her mad. "Malcolm!" she'd yell. "There's no blithering ice!"

"Are you okay?" Meredith stood in the kitchen. Diana clambered to her feet; she seemed to be sitting on the chair.

"I'm fine. Put the door back, will you?" She turned away, pulled off some kitchen roll and blew her nose. "Bloody house," she said, "there's all these little things, not quite big enough to get a builder in for."

"We have to do it ourselves," said Meredith, shoving back the door. "Women have to learn to live without men."

Diana thought: but I don't want to! She said: "Where's Zak?"

"In the pool."

"Should he be there alone?"

"He's fine." Meredith took the tray. "I'll carry that."

Diana thought churlishly: You don't need a man because you're almost one yourself. If Malcolm were here they could say it to each other, giggling guiltily and shutting each other up. She couldn't possibly say this to anyone else.

The phone rang. It was Francine, Meredith's girlfriend. Diana felt another spasm of irritation. Couldn't she have Meredith to herself, just for a few hours? She got irritable so easily nowadays, the slightest thing set it off. People made allowances in the first few months but she really must try to pull herself together. A weeping widow – they could cope with that. But most of grief's manifestations were so unattractive – irritability, slow wits, resentment against all the second-rate people in the world who stayed alive.

She looked at Meredith's broad back; she wore a t-shirt and baggy, vaguely army trousers. "Shall we go ahead and make an offer?" Meredith was discussing a flat she was buying with Francine. Diana knew she should be more interested in this – an involved mother discussing curtains. But she only thought: in a few months Meredith and Zak will be living in a place Malcolm's never seen. Each day, of course, brought more of these things. Soon she herself was going to have to buy a new car, her Renault was falling to bits, and start driving around in something that had no connection with him whatsoever. She thought: I must ask him what sort of car to buy. Then she realised – how stupid!

She carried the tray into the garden. She walked down to the pool. Zak lay floating in the water. He lay face down, motionless.

Diana laid the tray on the grass – look, quite calmly! She kicked off her espadrilles, strode to the pool and jumped in. The water closed over her head.

She surfaced, spluttering, and lunged towards her grandson. She grabbed his shoulder; they bumped together and sank. He struggled – he was surprisingly strong – and when he surfaced he yelled: "Help!"

Diana felt her clothes ballooning around her. Zak's wiry arm grabbed her. "Hey!" she spluttered, pushing it off.

She swam to the edge and heaved herself up the steps, gasping for breath. Zak pulled himself up behind her.

"Mum!" he called. Meredith was running across the grass. "I saved Granny! She jumped into the pool!"

Diana tried to speak but she had a fit of coughing.

"She was trying to drown!" he gasped.

Meredith grabbed a towel. She rubbed Diana briskly. "Shall I take off your dress?" she asked. "Are you all right?"

"I wasn't trying to kill myself," said Diana, catching her breath. "I was trying to rescue Zak."

"Why?" asked Zak.

"You were drowning."

"I was counting worms," he said.

"What?"

"I was counting all the dead worms lying on the bottom of the pool."

Meredith's hands stopped. There was a moment's silence, then Diana found she was making a noise. For a moment she didn't recognise it; it felt like a rusty door opening in her chest. She was laughing.

Even Meredith smiled. Zak gazed at them dispassionately. Diana grabbed the towel and rubbed her hair vigorously. Suddenly she felt full of energy; refreshed by her dip in the water, she felt more wide awake than she had felt for months.

"You're shivering," said Meredith.

"I'm fine," she said. "I just thought – I've lost one man, I don't want to lose another."

Zak got up and slid back into the pool. Diana lay on the grass and let the sun warm her through her wet dress. Meredith said: "Yesterday a car stopped outside our flat. It was the same as Dad's Rover, and covered in mud. I thought: he's going to get out. He's going to ring the bell and say *I've been on this long journey, look at the milometer. But I'm back now.*"

There was a long silence. In the lilac bush a blackbird sang. Meredith said: "The reason I didn't want to swim is I've got so fat."

"Since he died, you mean," said Diana.

Meredith nodded. "And you didn't swim because you've got so thin." She paused. "How are you, Mum?"

And Diana told her.

Black Cherries

Olivia Davison

To:
His Honour Judge Edmund Jenkins Q.C.
Blake House Chambers
London 1st October 1995

There is not much light in my room. The shadows are the colour of my clothes. I crouch near to the paper so that I can see my words as they fall from my pen. I want *you* to see my words. I want you to hold this paper in your hand and stare at it with desperate eyes; prisoners looking for a door the way I have looked for a door and now have found one.

I want to hurt you the way you hurt others. Does that scare you? Are you a coward with veins full of milk, curdling inside as I tell you "the game is up"?

Of course this is not a game. I am serious. I dress in black and sit at my desk in the middle of an empty room before I write to you. The desk is small and square, a fragile antique, the top shaped in wafer-thin sheets of bird's eye maple. It is light and vulnerable, as I have been vulnerable, an easy target for your shots. My desk is bare save for a few sheets of parchment and a crystal bottle that I have filled with ink the colour of eyes. Ebony eyes dark as coal, indignant, and proud, eyes that glare with a blue blackness, never scared, glistening, impossible to intimidate. I have envied such eyes. My pen is balanced on the bottle, the gold nib a nugget in this dark, shining, it rocks like a bird pecking at the page, it is eager to begin.

These are the tools of my trade. I am industrious, a diligent craftsman honing my sentences, assembling in strings of pearl-black words the thoughts that I want you to share. I do not write to you hastily. I practise for hours scrawling sentences full of judgement verbs, adjectives of recrimination, and then I start again. I temper my prose in an effort to deceive you longer, hunched over my desk I appear a nervous scholar, rejecting my words, tearing my pages until they lie like shavings, litter around my feet. Only when I am knee-deep in a snow of ill-constructed menace am I happy with my work. Then I rise, kiss my envelope, and spilling my saliva in wasted trails, I seal this letter for you.

I want you to know as you read it the care I have taken and the care I will take to destroy you.

I am always sad. My thoughts circle in this gloom like bats, blind and helpless they bang around in my head, upsetting me, knocking over thoughts of your selfishness. My brain swills in the oil of your malice, my body marinates as it spreads, seeping into me, finding my veins, filling the wrinkles in my skin until the spill happens and swollen globules of my grief drop from the nib of my pen, saturating the paper I have bought especially for you.

Do not laugh at me. I know it is mourning paper, pages edged in black for use by grieving relatives, but I felt it appropriate. I have as much grief within me as the bereaved. I want you to know about it. I want you to imagine me as I sit here alone. I want you to come and chatter in my silence. Sitting in my room like an uncaged bird I want you to sing for me.

I am tired of being alone. Tired of not having. This more than anything else, even more than your behaviour, has caused me to write to you.

*

I know about you. I know where you go. I know everything you do in the dirty hidden corners of your life. I see you as you bend in twisted positions, squatting on her like a dog, jabbing at her in the dark of a black back alley. I can smell the humiliation as you poke and thrust, grunting your satisfaction in a cramped front seat, the only space in your affair.

I am a collector in a hood. With hands outstretched I wait for you.

The cost of your deceit is high. Perhaps too high, for I do not know how much you earn. I cannot say if you will be able to meet my demands. I do not care, there is a lack of emotion in my world, which reduces your plight to a nothingness. If the money I demand does not arrive I will not be affected but your wife will know, and she will be injured, injured enough to tell others. I will send her copies of this and every other letter that I write. For her I will use scented paper, the sort that smells of violets. Does your wife like flowers? Can you remember?

I am sorry. I am a romantic. My nature dictates the location. Leave the sum of £1000.00 behind the blue girder in the bandstand in the park at 4.00 p.m. on Friday.

Thank you for reading my words. It is important to me that you read them.

To:
His Honour Judge Edmund Jenkins Q.C.
Blake House Chambers
London 7th October 1995

I have spent your money. I know it has not lasted long but I will be more careful in the future. I am afraid it went to my head. The waste of your money that is. I know you are careful with money. I know how you finger it in your trousers, pressed into your wallet like a rare flower collection, I know it comforts you. It is not my fault I am writing these letters. I am helpless in the face of such injustice. I know that the night you left the money at the bandstand you saw her again.

You have changed your location but I tracked you, standing in the shadows I wore the clothes I wear when I write to you. I covered my face in the folds of my cloak as you hung her over a front seat and toyed with her. You buried your face in her, searching, I imagine, for the reason you were there.

You must not think me prudish, there is nothing wrong with lust. I myself am guilty of outrageous behaviour beside which your antics seem like a toe in the water, the tight constrained motions of a nun. Trembling fantasies have driven me to sex, cravings deeper than your wildest imaginings have opened me up, deep groans of satisfaction I have roared through open windows from wrecked beds draped in silk, cowering in the dark listening to your snorts I have cringed at the comparison, understanding then the smallness of your mind.

I have been eaten alive by passion. It happened in France. I was too old for intrigue but such things are not planned. I was not supposed to be in France, I was supposed to be elsewhere, completely elsewhere, another country in fact but I needed to be alone. I abandoned everything in my life and went to France. I spent two days and one night away from my family and I discovered love. Not a roll in the dirt with a drunken tart and a few juddering movements but hours and hours of satisfaction.

It started when a woman fed me cherries. She was flagrant. I knew she wanted me from the moment she introduced herself. We sat in a café shaded by the trees, a hot wind blew from the fields and she smiled at me. The blue checked tablecloths shaking as she walked between them. We were alone in the café as she introduced herself and in the silence of the afternoon fed me cherries. Leaning across the table, her blouse half open, her breasts pressing on my arm she leaned into my life. I remember the way the cherries hung in front of my lips before I caught them and burst them open between my tongue and my teeth. Prodding their soft flesh I skewered them and spat their insides in an ashtray. As I write I can taste their juice. The taste of her savoured on my lips easing my memory, a palliative in a box of bitter pills which you have fed me. In front of my eyes is the image of their skin, black and polished as this mail. The skin split and the soft pink flesh revealed, the contrast too great for one lifetime.

Leave me more money. £5000.00 this time in the same place.

I don't think the Lord Chancellor tolerates adulterers in the Family Court.

To:
His Honour Judge Edmund Jenkins Q.C.
Blake House Chambers
London 27th November 1995

I am sorry I have not been in touch. Did you think I had gone away? I apologise if you were lonely. It is truly awful to be lonely. I know. I have been lonely all my life. I think people are lonely when they are not understood. It is all right being in a crowded room but no good at all if you are Russian and everyone is talking Gaelic and sharing views on the price of haggis.

Have you ever felt like that, or are you one of those lucky people who has always fitted in? Do you ever sit on the floor in the corner of a room and screw yourself up into a ball so you can hug yourself and not fall off the earth? I suppose not. I forgot you were invulnerable.

I am sorry I am rambling. I have been drinking and I cannot write. My words are coming out as gibberish and I know you are ashamed of them.

I know you don't like fools or drunks.

I am delighted to write to you as both.

More money please. £5000.00 was a better amount than £1000.00. It felt more comforting.

Do you know if I wasn't drunk I would swear today is the day that the Family Law bill goes before Parliament. Do you think mediation will affect the number of judges they need?

To:
His Honour Judge Edmund Jenkins Q.C.
Blake House Chambers
London 28th November 1995

I have had the blackest day. I woke up and I knew there was no point to my existence. All the air seemed choked with hopelessness. I dressed in red but I could not hide my sorrow. My eyes show what my life has done to me and as I walk my sadness weights my shoes, slowing me down. To cheer myself up I went to a flower shop, but all they had were peonies, black as ravens they hung their heads over the side of my bag wilting as I breathed on them.

As I climbed the steps of the bandstand I felt your presence. At first I thought you were watching and I drew back inside my hood. I proceeded cautiously, checking the air for the smell of you, but when I opened the bag I realised it was only your words strapped to my cash that infected the space, intimidating me.

I am appalled by your note. I had heard you were the sort to make threats. I think you fail to realise that I have the upper hand. I don't mind if you do not pay. What does it matter to me if you involve the police? So much the better. I will either empty your pockets of your wealth, or spend a life in jail writing about your sordid nature. Either way you will be ruined, either way I will be happy. You must realise you cannot hurt me. I am beyond your venom.

Because you have tried to intimidate me and although I do not like to use the term, “bully me into submission”, I would like you to leave £20,000 by tomorrow afternoon.

To:
His Honour Judge Edmund Jenkins Q.C.
Blake House Chambers
London 29th November 1995

Thank you. I am sorry if my tone seemed sharp. Obviously in view of the amount you will not be hearing from me for some time.

To:
His Honour Judge Edmund Jenkins Q.C.
Blake House Chambers
London 11th December 1995

I am sorry, I know you will be irritated to hear from me so soon. It is just that I have had the most marvellous idea and I am so excited that I wanted to share it with you. I am in such a rush to communicate with you I have not even dressed myself up to write. My cloak is at my feet and the curtains are open. I feel I can communicate with you, almost without pretending, which is an enormous advance. In fact I feel much brighter generally, although I don’t like to think it is anything to do with the increasing balance in my bank account.

I have decided to reform myself. I do not want to be a criminal. I want to put it all behind me and start over, my criminal career that is. I have an offer to make you. Pay me the sum of £50,000 and you will never hear from me again.

I know you don’t believe me, and I accept I have not always kept my word in the past, but you see I have a settled intention to start over. A new life. I am suddenly so full of energy I believe I can live a life like everyone else. PLEASE TRUST ME. LEAVE THE MONEY TOMORROW 4.00 p.m. AND WE WILL BOTH BE FREE. NO MORE THREATS.

To:
His Honour Judge Edmund Jenkins
Blake House Chambers
London 12th December 1995

Are you trembling as you read this letter? I am trembling as I think of you reading it. A thousand miles from you and still I am affected. Have you opened the curtains in my room? Holding my cloak, do you tap on my desk considering your revenge? I can imagine your anger, circling inside you, trapped by the strait-jacket of your feelings, eating away at your heart in your unemotional life.

You will be white with aggression as you consider how I could do this, but the truth is you have made me very unhappy. At first I did not think you intended to but as the years passed I understood I was part of your sport. I do not know if you realise the effect your disapproval had on me. At first I was indifferent, but then the odd word caught in my hair, clinging to me like rags to a hedge, until I was so covered in insults I could not find myself any more. I forgot what I looked like when you married me, and worse still I forgot who I was.

A thousand dinner parties have passed since we met, a million sips of liqueur stagnant on my lips remind me of your venom. When you sneered at me your lips would harden, tightening against me, against the error of your choice. You made a mistake, you thought I was someone else and for twenty years you made me pay. I had no allies, our friends were in your camp, the women fawning, believing you would not sneer at them, the men condoning, appreciating you had a lot to put up with as I tripped on chipped heels and staggered for my bedroom, clutching my gin and leaving the tonic behind.

Words are weapons. More violent than guns. Ripping through skin, by-passing flesh, ignoring the larger fighting self, they hit their target at the core, the small and nervous being, only just breathing, they kill at birth. Ricocheting from the centre they devastate and leave, the cruellest mercenaries, unaccountable, invisible, unlicensed.

I am glad *my* words have been able to intimidate you.

Words which at first were shy. Frightened words, scratched in the dark under my cloak, finding their true nature began to dance, becoming bold and loud as they injured you.

I did not care that you had an affair. I did not care that in your arrogance you did not hide the snail trail of lust which led me to your car. I want you to know that I am overwhelmingly delighted that you needed yet another woman. So close to home. So indifferent to my pain I was able to catch you. Your deceit has set me free. Your weakness in the face of my demands has bought me a life so far away you will never be able to touch me.

I have gone. Thank you for the money. I wanted you to understand why I treated you in this way, and it is only now that I am out of your house and free of you that I am able to tell you the words I have kept in my head for years.

I do not imagine you will ever try to find me. You have never cared for me and I know you could not live with the shame if you involved the police but should you wonder where I am, think only this: against all odds, life for some can be a bowl of cherries, black, but cherries nevertheless.

Yours no longer,
Alicia

Pyramid

Erica Wagner

On a moonless night the Pyramid hides behind a wall of onyx. The desert night drops down like a hawk and swallows the city, the river, the sea of sand all around and makes them as if they never were. Even in the palace the islands of light are few, and in between them the corridors open up to the thick blackness without walls or floors or windows. It's all the same, cavelike. Some people say you can vanish altogether on these nights: your hand disappears in front of your face and you go mad with imagining its outline, and by the time the light comes you are gone and no one can find you. My nurse used to tell me this to make me go to sleep, to stop me climbing into the seat by my window and watching the shimmering black. On these nights with no moon the light from the stars stops far short of the ground and hangs like a distant celebration at which no one is welcome, at which even the daughters of kings are not welcome. My father is the King. But the night hides nothing; not any more.

At dusk the Great Pyramid begins to lose its shape. In the red light the edges of the stone seem to bleed out into the sand so that the two become one: a huge square-shouldered dune in the dying light. The sand laps against the base of the stone like the river laps against the bank, eating away at it, rubbing the corners smooth. There was gossip among the masons that the base would be quite worn down before the top was even begun. They had time to gossip, as they stood by the quay waiting for the barges of stone to arrive – which came less and less often, as everyone knew. Everyone in the palace, and in the city too, I am sure: for the city is nothing now but a great machine to grind out men for the use of the King. If a family has two sons, one will go to work on the Pyramid; if three, two must be sent to haul stone. He who fathers four sons will send two to build, and one to serve in the garrison when he comes of age. This is the law. It is read out in the public squares by the crier who blows on his trumpet and calls, The Pharaoh is merciful and kind: the Son of the Sun spares each family a boy to till the fields: the people will never be hungry. The Pharaoh is merciful and kind: the Son of the Sun builds his monument to his glory which is the glory of the kingdoms over which he rules: from the tomb his perfected spirit will protect and bless his people, who send their sons to build in his name. The Pharaoh blesses his people while yet he lives: the Pharaoh blesses his people in the glory of his death.

I could hear it from my window. But I thought the people must be hungry: in the palace there was much spice but little meat, and what there was had maggots beyond spicing. The grain had the smell of cellars about it. I grew thin. If I lay on my back I could feel the hollow in my belly, and cup my hands around the hummocks of bone that rose at the level of my hips. Not that I've ever been much bigger. My nurse used to say I was scrawny, and make me drink the fatty cream that swirled on top of the milk. I would never find a husband, she would say, and we would laugh. I am betrothed to my cousin, my father's sister's son. We played together as children, but now I do not see him much. When I asked my nurse why she shrugged and said, soon you will be weary enough of the sight of his face.

Since I was born, the river has risen sixteen times. And sixteen times it has risen since the King my father decreed that his Pyramid should be begun. We have grown together.

Because the Pyramid was always there, it was easy not to notice it. I never thought of it, any more than I would think of the nose on my face when I looked in my silver mirror.

Of course, I heard it discussed. If I sat with my father I would hear extravagant compliments made to it, comparisons drawn, and would see the King's fine mouth turned in smiling, his white teeth bared as he spoke delightedly of this weight of stone, of that number of men, of his Chief Mason, born in the slums of Cairo but whom the Pharaoh loved as his son. All this I heard; and all this I ignored, as I sat on an ebony stool at my father's feet with my hands in my lap, twisting the scarab on my finger. It was hard to recall, with his eyes so dark and alive, that my father was speaking of his death. Then he would be King forever. This was what he wanted most. It was the mason who could grant him his wish.

The Pyramid kept to itself. It grew out in the desert, where it was necessary to peer hard to see its white surface swarming with men so that it seemed to be covered with a veil that rippled in the hot breeze. I looked at it very rarely. It is such a vast thing, its growth so slow – like the growth of a child – that daily observance is not rewarding. Once a year, maybe less, maybe more, I might look out and think, it has grown by the length of the last joint of my finger (my hand held out to the horizon, one eye shut against the sun). Don't stare out at the sand, said my nurse. You'll get a squint.

And so I would listen to her, and look away. Night would come, and seal the desert up, releasing only the clatter of the kites as they fought over something discarded. I hear they do not bury the bodies of the labourers who fall in the service of the tomb, that the sun and the kites take them quickly enough. The sand must be scattered with bones, sown lightly into the ground like seeds strewn on a field. When did I first think such a thing? Not so long ago. I can't remember, exactly. But I began to have nightmares, and my father's tomb began to be something no longer quite forgotten; a whisper in my ear or a footstep too close in the dark.

Not long after my dreaming began, the cargoes of stone stopped altogether.

Late one night, the Pharaoh came to see me. He drew the curtain of my chamber and stood in the little light that flickered out from a brazier by the door. My nurse, who was seated by my bed, dropped to her knees and put her face to the ground in front of the god.

I was not quite asleep. I opened my eyes, and did not move.

The Pharaoh put out his hand to my nurse, for she is not young, to lift her up. In these small ways my father is a simple man: he will do the necessary thing.

"You will leave us," he said to her, and she nodded, and went towards her chamber, which is through a little door by the foot of my bed. The King held up his arm to block her passage, and she looked up into his face, so startled was she. "Leave us alone," he said. And so she backed out of the chamber and into the dark hall. I heard her steps for a long time. I often wonder, now, if she knew he would come. I used to think she knew all such things.

When she had gone, he came and sat on the edge of my bed, a thing he had never done before. One leg he drew in close to his body, and the other he stretched out on the floor; his sandal slid off and he flexed his bare foot. I sat up. I was glad to see him.

"My lord," I said.

He said nothing, but lifted his hand to touch my hair, and looked down at me, and in his face was something I had never seen, a private face not exposed to ministers and servants, and kept well away from the sculptors who make him impassive and beautiful. The skin beneath his eyes looked fragile, and below the lashes of one I could see a little blue vein that beat fast, like the heart of a bird. His linen shirt was not clean. For a moment I almost wondered if I was myself, if he was the Pharaoh, or if we had been shifted into some other life where we might sit like this together as if it were our custom. But it was not so.

He opened his mouth as if to speak, but made no sound, and shut it. One hand he kept on my head, in my hair, pulling it through his fingers, through his fist, and the other hand lay like a dead thing in his lap, weighted with gold. His eyes looked into mine, but the oil lamp cast a sheen across their surface through which I could not see. Then he twisted his neck, looked away, out the window to the desert, where the Pyramid breathed the day's heat back out into the night.

When he turned and stood, I saw his statue-face, the god's face, and I bent my head against its stare. I did not see his hand reach down to grasp the corner of the sheet that covered me, but felt the air cool on my body as he drew it quickly down to the foot of the bed.

I was naked, except for the knotted necklace that was once my mother's. I lifted a hand to cover myself, but the King took my wrist in his grasp to stop me. I closed my eyes, and heard his breath. When he spoke he was smiling; it was in the slant of his voice.

"The Pharaoh's daughter is beautiful," he said.

I opened my eyes. And saw his face change again, felt him draw up the sheet fast to my neck and put his hand on my mouth to stop what words might come, but there were none to be stopped. He kissed my forehead, and then rose and turned his back and left.

Nothing was different; and nothing was the same. When my nurse returned, I lay still as if I were asleep, but through half-closed eyes could see the light of the waxing moon, and the shadow of the Pyramid stretched across the sand.

Three days after the King's night visit, I returned to my chamber to find, not my nurse: another woman, younger, with a proud neck and many jewels. I said to her, where is my nurse? I want my nurse here – and I stood very straight because I am the daughter of the King and she was to me nothing. But she looked at me with black eyes that saw no princess, and she laughed. She stepped forward, so that the little bells on her ankles chimed, and she said, I am your nurse now. And she kissed me. But her eyes never left my face, and my heart went hard inside my chest. We said nothing else: she undressed me, and sat at my side, and again I lay and did not sleep.

Or thought I did not: but in the morning I was awakened by her ringing feet. She laughed again when she saw my open eyes, and I wondered that she always laughed.

"My princess!" she said, and clapped her hands together. I sat up, and she ran to me, carrying in her arms a dress of rich silk dyed indigo, which she laid against my shoulder. It was soft as fur, like nothing I had ever worn.

"Do you like it?" she asked eagerly, her voice low as if we were playing a game together. "It is beautiful, isn't it?" She touched my face, my shoulder, with the back of her hand, her rings cool against my skin.

"Is it mine?" I asked, and she nodded as if just that thought made her happier than she could bear, and pulled me up with both of her pretty hands to dress me in it and brush my hair. It was a complicated shift of pleats and folds, and as she moved me this way and that her look was the look of the Pharaoh, as he'd stood that night by the foot of my bed.

The mason's name is Selket. He saw me in the indigo dress and he smiled, and touched the skin of my shoulder with his fingertips. When my pretty nurse said to me, Selket, the Chief Mason, is here to see the Princess, I did not know why. I imagined some matter of state. I imagined the Pharaoh was ill. I wondered why there was not some minister to see the Pharaoh's favourite. I wondered this until I felt the mason's calloused hands.

It was after noon when he arrived; the sun had not yet set when he left. Before he turned to go, he took from a pocket of his robe two little gold hoops set with turquoise beads, and when I would not take them from him, he set them on the table by the bed, and bent and kissed my cheek. He is not an unkind man. I know that now.

My nurse came and bathed me. I did not move: I let her lift my arms and pull the rings from my fingers as if I were to be laid out for embalming. Her face was smiling, as it ever was, but the smile was painted on like a mask, and she spoke very little. When I am with them, she sits behind a curtain and listens.

Before I went to bed that night, I spoke to her. She was standing by the window of her chamber, combing her thick hair, and she did not hear me come in. She must have thought I was asleep. Her face was clean of paint, and in the moonlight it looked almost plain.

"Do not tell me their names," I said. "Selket's name I know, and that is enough. Do not tell me anything about them." I held out the little gold earrings the mason had given me, and she took them, and looked down at them as if she had never seen any such thing. "There is only one thing I ask," I said. "Only one gift. Tell them that the Pharaoh's daughter has as her price what the Pharaoh so desires himself. I will accept nothing else."

I left her standing with the jewels in her palm, and returned to my bed. Before the week was out, the Pyramid was darkened again with swarms of men, straining to draw the great stones up towards the sun.

It was Selket, of course, who first understood. Strange gifts came with stranger men: rich men bearing statues of Maat, with her feather of the soul, of Anubis and his scales, gifts of immortality. I made them take these away. Whatever I had become, I found that in the words of the Pharaoh's daughter there was still some power. But one afternoon Selket opened the curtain of my chamber, and sat down on my bed as the Pharaoh had. His face is made almost black from his years in the sun, his skin is creased and leathery.

But the whites of his eyes are clear and bright, and when the dark pupils glitter like the eyes of a hawk, this means his smile will follow. He has more teeth than the usual.

One hand he took from behind his back and pulled me closer to him. Then he took my wrist and turned it, so my upraised palm was held out to him.

"I have brought you a gift," he said.

"The earrings you gave me were very beautiful," I said. "My serving woman wears them. What have you brought me now?"

Boldness comes easily from my mouth now. Some other place inside of me has opened: it comes from there, like a second voice.

"I have brought what I bring for the Pharaoh. What he buys with his most precious of jewels."

Selket kissed the palm of my hand. He grows bald at the top of his head. Then he took from behind him a small block of stone, small enough for me to hold in one hand, neatly cut, with sharp, square corners.

Rumour takes word of Selket's gift and sets it loose like a bird about the city. So now my little pyramid rises, slowly, like its great father out in the sand. With each gift of stone it grows, the blocks so prettily and carefully cut that I wonder if it is not the Chief Mason himself who carves them.

But Selket I no longer see. Perhaps he is no longer the favourite of the King. It does not matter. Only the Pyramid matters: a living thing in the desert, a twin I never knew I had. No one, I think, will build my tomb. Tell them this: that when I die, I would not have my body dried and bound, but taken out to the desert, to the foot of my father's mountain. Leave me to lie where I belong, among the bodies of the men who built it, whose bones rattle in the hot wind.

Rhubarb

Susan Holland

Phoebe isn't going to wait for them to come back for lunch. She's already served up. Rhubarb soup, in the garden. All the different parts of the meal are made of rhubarb. Placemats of whole rhubarb leaf. Soup dishes of half rhubarb leaf. Croutons of rhubarb stalk which she's tried in vain to break into smaller pieces. She's bent them and twisted them but the stalks are strong. The legs of a doll with long flexed calves and tapering Cinderella feet.

Phoebe is not one to give up. She is in a trance of activity. She's forgotten what it was she set out to do. When success ceases to matter the stalk she is working on amazingly perforates right across and a clear jelly appears at the site of the injury like the watery stuff on a cut knee. Her hair starts to bother her. The curls around her hairline wriggle with sweat. She brushes her hair off her face with the back of her arm like a harassed domestic worker. A great voluptuous gesture. With a further sort of jaundiced swagger she's picked up somewhere or other, she balances all her weight on one hip and looks around for a suitable tool to finish off the job with the rhubarb.

The minute her parents arrive, they're away out again. Phoebe stays with her grandparents at the bungalow. Her parents need to be with one another, on their own. It's something they can't do in London. But they set out together and come back separately, through the fence or by the gate. The front or the back.

The front is exposed. There is a steep drop, its edge

disguised by bracken; below is a beach striped like Fair Isle knitting, the sewage pipe wriggling through camomile daisies and the sea shrinking, or slopping, in the bay. Phoebe watches her parents from the front till they round the point. Her mother dragging, or chasing, her father along the shore. Her father behind, or in front of her mother. Her father stopping to look at something on the beach, her mother catching up with him, her father taking off like a wading bird, never flying away completely but settling again along the beach.

The back feels safe. More sheltered. Its pink pebbledash is like a grazed knee. Here are the rhubarb beds, grey dustbins with tarry caps like jackdaws, a circular clothes line with sagging wires of saffron yellow, and rowan trees. A mile away, on the town green, is the faint outline of the bunjie-jumping crane which is there for three days only. If she stood between the dustbins she could even see the spider people jumping. Their shouts carry across the loch. Her father may be taking her to watch, tomorrow.

Her grandparents may be watching her now. But she can't see them. The windows are the colour of peat. In her parents' bedroom window, the mirror is the shape of a pirate hat.

"Is she all right?" calls her grandfather.

"I think so." Her grandmother lowers her voice because Phoebe is right outside.

"Little soul," he adds, as if he's sorry for her.

Phoebe changes her plans. When she realises more work is needed on the stalk to break the shreds, she loses interest and makes it into something else. The loop of cellulose fibre is resilient as hair. The hair is rainbow-coloured and grows out of two different extremities, jumps the gap like electrical wires and joins in the middle. The threads have a sticky brightness like doll hair.

She needs more rhubarb for something. Rhubarb is a safe choice. She isn't allowed to pick anything else in the garden but she is allowed to pull the rhubarb. After July,

Granny says, it is poisonous! She enjoys pulling the rhubarb so much she can't really believe it is allowed. She hangs onto a rhubarb plant leaning back with all her weight and pulling with all her strength which is phenomenal for six. At the same time she watches the kitchen window where any moment Granny's white perm might drift across like a jellyfish and a face form smiling vaguely like the moon. But the moon fails to make an appearance in the window. The window-panes of the bungalow hold a caving reflection of blank sky. It makes her imagine rainbow colours, chalky pastel rays like Edinburgh rock. Since no one is evidently going to stop her Phoebe carries on pulling rhubarb, her palms sliding on a pink and green satiny stalk.

Phoebe is getting frustrated. She tries a number of rhubarb stalks and they all stay rooted. They sway, carve the soil into shallow moats around them and resist. She is on her father's shoulders. Leaning back far enough to make him protest. But the rhubarb neck is unresponsive. Every time she pauses and rests, she fiddles with a loose tooth.

It is not sore. She thinks: so this is what it's like to have a loose tooth! The tooth is a small point of hope in a great wasteland of time to be crossed, a prickle of stimulation. At last something's happening. And it's easy to cope with. I'm good at having a loose tooth. But what if the swaying tooth never comes out?

Phoebe squats, throws back her head and tries again. She sees a crow flying over and disappearing into the black cumulus of gorse which edges the bank. She stops for a moment and looks at the window.

When Dad is absent the void fills with God, little bits of God everywhere like the freezing hot spray from a can of deodorant. God is a handsome young male with eyes like a cat. He runs away unless you approach him on bended knees, darts into bushes with all four legs moving like a centipede if you bungle it and call him too enthusiastically or try to seize him. Sometimes if you get it right he glides round your breath-held form or sniffs your fingers. On rare occasions he reduces you to helpless giggles as he quests for salt on your skin with his tongue as rough as a fruit pastille. But he can't be commanded, he comes and goes to please himself, stays or stays away.

Phoebe has got a postcard for her friend in London, from the Whimbrel gift shop in the harbour. A golden eagle pulling the intestine (or something) out of a mush of brown fur. She has examined the picture closely, trying to identify the different bits. Her rhubarb stalk is a talon. Emerging stupidly out of its frilly green shirt. Her culottes flap. She is sitting on her father's shoulders. She is trying to close up the gap between her knees. He is looking annoyed and trying to stop her throttling him. He is warning her to sit properly or she'll have to come down.

"I'm going to chop you up and feed you to my babies," Phoebe tells the rhubarb.

Phoebe succeeds in pulling out the rhubarb, the whole lot with the root. She staggers backwards looking helplessly at the uprooted rhubarb tree. Her head spins and her body is dust.

This is how she used to feel when she was little. After her father took her off his shoulders and set her down to walk by herself. As he made to pick up Phoebe her mother always tried to stop him anyway, saying, "Oh, no, you'll break your back. Phoebe, you're too big!"

She squats right down around her next plant for better leverage and agitates it along with her tooth. She is suspended from the plant and buoyed up by it. She rides it. It has huge exhilarating strides. She is off again. Again her life is filled with automatic busyness.

Between efforts at the rhubarb Phoebe pushes with her tongue against the tooth. Every bout of activity with her tongue is risky and irresistible. As she pulls she clenches her teeth together to keep them in her gums and as she relaxes she jiggles the tooth to assess the amount of damage done.

*

Phoebe can now pick her mother up. If she pushes her head between her mother's legs she can raise her for a moment off the floor. And even stagger a few steps. The first time she did it her mother gasped, "You really make me laugh!" – exclaiming at her helplessly loosening legs. Afterwards Phoebe's mother's face, which is normally strained, was red and beaming. Phoebe decided then to make her mother laugh as often as she could.

She has tried to repeat the coup. It has never been so successful as the first time. If her mother's back is turned, say, washing the dishes, she is at risk of Phoebe trying to pick her up. "You really make me laugh," Phoebe prompts her hopefully. But her mother sidesteps her irritably. Grandad says that what is funny the first time doesn't stay funny. This morning he said, "Mummies don't like horseplay, do they Phoebe?"

"No, really, it's the Daddies who like to romp," he explained to Phoebe's mother. "Women on the whole don't really enter into physical games with children."

"Lack of imagination?" her mother snarled. "Men are all children at heart!"

"Sure as eggs is eggs you're going to end up alone with that attitude!"

Then her mother suddenly straddled Phoebe and pinned her down. Phoebe shrieked. Grandad said, "Shh!"

Breakfast was over. Grandad was preparing a meal for the birds from crumbs of leftover toast. It was the only food he did prepare. He hurled a fistful of crumbs out of the window and the back garden was suddenly full of sounds, wings and crackling twigs.

"Granny!" Phoebe's grandfather calls. Her grandmother is clamping a can of beans onto the can-opener. She leaves the can suspended. The wee glistening puncture spreads into a smelly ring and drowns the lid.

Phoebe's grandfather appears in the garden, thumping the breast of his wind-cheater looking for the lump made by his hanky and shaking it out like a conjurer. He ushers Phoebe into the porch, standing with his hands on Phoebe's shoulders as if to say, "For pity's sake, do something!" to Phoebe's grandmother. Then takes on the job himself. A hot face-cloth treatment for Phoebe's missing tooth. The face-cloth rough and salving as the tongue of a cat.

Phoebe's parents have come back together for once. They are suddenly there, struggling with the doors in the airtight porch and wobbling on loosened wellingtons. They look flustered and guilty. Phoebe's grandfather says, "Don't lean on the glass you two. Goodness, even Phoebe knows better than to do that, don't you Phoebe?!"

Phoebe's cheeks are taut from the water.

"It might break, mightn't it, Grandad?"

He ignores her.

"Can I help you Mum?" says her mother.

"Uh, uh."

Granny upends the bean can into a saucepan. The beans come out in a crumbling lump like a failed sand-castle. Gritty drips squirt on the non-stick lining of the pan, then the rest in a farting rush.

"Now," says Phoebe's grandfather, having shut the door behind him, "never mind about your silly disagreements. Do you know what's happened to your little girl while you've been out, Mummy?"

Grandad likes to say exactly what the relationship is between all the members of the family. What everyone's title is.

"She's just lost a tooth. Is it her first?"

His voice sinks sympathetically into the word "tooth". Phoebe's mother shakes her head and squints down her nose in a long-sighted way but Phoebe teases her mother. She won't open up her mouth to let her mother see. She turns her face away like a baby.

Phoebe's mother looks like a harassed woman. As if she was interrupted planning to have a quiet smoke. Everyone seems to be watching them together. There's a second's hush before a clatter of distraction. Phoebe's grandfather starts to drum on the work-surface with his fingertips summoning lunch, her grandmother nudges the grill pan.

"Come on out of the way you two," she tells Phoebe and her mother.

The partition door opens and shuts several times, quietly but slow, like stage whispers. Phoebe's Dad takes his place last and is served first. "Talk about favouritism!" says Grandad. "Don't tell me we don't treat our visitors well."

Then he says to Phoebe's mother, "It's a joke! Do I have to signpost everything for you?"

Phoebe's grandmother says, "Did you see anybody then while you were down on the shore?"

The conversation jumps like someone avoiding puddles. Finding the dry spines of clumps of grass. Wobbly as skates.

"I don't think we saw a soul, did we?" Her mother looks at Phoebe's father politely. "We went fast. On the way back."

"Oh. Only a whilk-picker. He said 'morning', then he changed it into 'afternoon'!"

Phoebe is astonished. "I didn't know whilk-pickers could speak!"

Her grandmother gives her a slow frowning smile. "Oh Phoebe, what do you think whilk-pickers are?"

Everyone is laughing kindly.

They might be comical but oystercatchers aren't friendly. However far you walk along the shore they always stay ahead, jumping position like a rainbow's end. They like to look in the same direction, out to sea, or run on the wriggling silt behind a wave, but they don't mind how many times they have to fly away to keep their distance. Time after time, as people threaten to catch up with them, the flock is off, clamouring in phlegmatic rounds like an alarm clock, to settle for a temporary peace along the beach. But speak, no, grownups are fools, Phoebe hasn't heard one speak.

"She means oystercatchers," her mother explains, after everyone's stopped laughing.

"I didn't know daddies could speak!" says Phoebe. She only has to open her mouth. She can do it again, just say what comes into her head and it will be amazing!

"I didn't know table legs could speak!"

"I didn't know rissoles could speak!"

"I didn't know beans could speak!" That was the best one yet! She shakes with hilarity.

Her father stretches an arm across her mother to restrain Phoebe. But she's already racking her brains over the next one. She goes further afield for inspiration. "I didn't know teeth could go bunjie-jumping!" And she comes back flying. Everything's grist to her mill. There's no daft uncouth phrase she can't launch head first from a fifty-foot drop and it'll bounce back making Tarzan noises. She's there at the bunjie-jumping hurling words experimentally off the platform.

"I didn't know dogs could go bunjie-jumping!"

"I didn't know girls were allowed!"

"I didn't know . . ."

"Stop it, you're egging her on," says her father.

Her mother is smiling at Phoebe.

"Me. That's a turn-up for the books. I thought women never played with their children."

"You! Play! Do you know the meaning of the word?" says Phoebe's father.

"Do you understand now, Phoebe," asks her grandfather, "about the whilk-picker? Oystercatchers are birds and whilk-pickers are men."

"And women," her mother says.

Phoebe's father looks heavenwards.

He puts his hand up, pretending to be winding something.

He puts his hand down. He looks embarrassed. Phoebe's Granny offers him a Breakaway biscuit, from a tin.

Phoebe suddenly feels very very sorry for her father. She

goes to his place by the window and puts her arm around him. They fill up all the window-frame like a dressing table in a small room. Nothing much out there worth looking at, its position suggests, you might as well have this crouching room instead.

Phoebe's mother excuses her from the table. "The tooth fairy might come straight away if you go and have a nap now." And looks amazed when Phoebe goes.

Through the door Phoebe can hear a silence and she knows it is all her fault.

When Phoebe wakes she catches her mother in the act. Her mother is standing in the middle of Phoebe's bedroom. Like the hamster when you move the cage and put it down somewhere else and the hamster stays stock-still, hunched on the upper platform just looking ahead and trying to work out where it's landed up. Phoebe plays along with her mother.

"You're the tooth fairy really, aren't you Mum?"

Her mothers shakes her head in an embarrassed way. She comes and sits on the side of the bed. Sun is shining through the brown curtains. The room's turned pink. Phoebe sees her mother's eyes are snot-green.

Her mother explains that Daddy has had to go suddenly. When they go back to London Daddy will not be living with them any more. She opens the curtains and sits back down again.

Phoebe wants to go and play. But her mother is mumbling on. She is sorry etc. She doesn't know what to say. She doesn't know what will happen. She seems to be having difficulty breathing and there are long pauses between her observations. – She should have seen it coming.

Phoebe realises that you can actually see the bunjie-jumpers' crane from her bed. Over her mother's shoulder, through the window. The people go one at a time, like teeth, with long gaps between. They bounce a few times on a string then make a single cross shape on the sky – a kiss, as an afterthought, on a letter. It's a drag really. The pace of it is far too slow. You have to wait so long for something to happen and then you miss it when it does.

With Every Tick of the Heart

Candia McWilliam

The afternoon would not be moved. He smoked, she did her knitting, the cat sat waving his tail on top of the television, but nothing made the time pass. It was as though the air had braked, a great breath of afternoon had been taken and held. No person passed, either, outside the window of Denise and Norman's retirement apartment, on the corner of the busy shopping street and a quiet road full of dental surgeries. Denise and Norman rested in the still of the afternoon.

Their room was warmer than he liked it, but she suffered with cold hands and Petal liked the heat, too. Petal was a cat who would not go outside. His litter tray sat on the plastic drugget in the tiny hall and reeked. Norman emptied it once a week. Denise said she did it on the other days. He knew not to believe her, but it was easier to leave it. He indulged her like that, enjoying this late carelessness in their lives. From time to time he did not tidy the ashtray and his pipe of the night before, or they got silly together over gin and a box of Good News and as much Schubert as they could cram in, and failed to pick up the telephone if it rang, and slept in the next day. The days were brimming with a new timid freedom for the couple that made them unlike the other residents of these apartments. When time stood still they did not fret about it but admired the pose it struck. They were luxuriously idle, idle as teenagers with a meal of hours before them.

Norman was born to young parents, who raised him

with the casualness of confidence. His mother would eat off his plate and expected him to do the same to her. Neither parent was jealous of the kindness Norman showed to the other. Not counting up the favours bestowed by the baby, they took them for granted. Later Norman climbed up and down the kitchen dresser by the shelves, made jam tarts with his mother in sharp metal patty pans, and potty-trained himself throughout the summer of 1923, in the back garden of their cottage in Lancaster.

After the War, his father came home with a plate in his head and a limp. He couldn't settle but roamed around like a man hearing a fly and never coming upon it. He had a job in the bottle factory and Norman's mother worked in the haberdasher's further up the town, next door to the refreshment and tea shop. After her work was over, Norman sometimes went to collect her at the end of his day with the piano tuner and they might go into the tea shop.

"These aren't Stan's bottles," she often said, screwing the stony stopper into the dimpled glass of the lemonade bottle, "Stan's are for something stronger than the pop." They might have cold pie or they might have railway pudding, a big cube of dry yellow sponge in a bowl of custard whose level sank as the pudding fattened up.

"Just drinking up the custard," Peggy would say. "Listen to that pudding sup."

"She's a wise woman. Wise and good-looking."

An old man was talking to them. He sat down. He had on a tie and braces, buttoned to the trousers with leather ears. How did he get those trousers off? How could he pull them down without pulling his shoulders down too? Norman did not care to think about these things, but they just came to him, like the passing need he had had as a boy to say something rude about Jesus in Sunday School.

Not like Jesus, this man, as far as you could tell, though he seemed to have been there when the five thousand had been fed. Or he seemed to have stopped the five thousand getting a look in.

Now there was a lot of trifle on the table. In a bowl, on the table it glowed, covered with cream and sugar strands.

"No carrageen in that cream at all. All comes out of my girls," said the old man.

Norman's mother asked first. Luckily Norman had not got the picture in his mind fully in focus before his mother said, "Girls?"

"Gorgeous heifers. Just two. High yielding girls. They come in to be milked rolling full. Udders rocking with cream." He looked at Norman's mother most particularly pleasantly as he said it. She snapped her beads between the first two fingers of her right hand and said, "Perhaps for Norman's sake, I'll say yes. He never gets all that goodness."

"I am sure that's not so. I've particularly noticed you and young Norman here. You take care to feed him wholesome, and you must have eaten wholesome, to have kept yourself so."

Not vain about how she looked any more, Peggy was easy to flatter about her son. The move from vanity about one's own looks to those of one's children is biological, the first burning out and the second kindling with the first birth. Although Norman was by now a full-grown young man, his mother took the credit for his shining health just as though she still soaked his rusk for him each morning.

"I'm Ernest Cargill. Proprietor here. And at the garages on the road out of town. By the Maiden Hotel, where I also preside." He made himself sound like an enormous hen, crouching low over his eggs.

"Interested in motors?" Ernest Cargill asked Norman.

"I hope to be a piano tuner. I'm apprenticed."

"There's one thing you need for that job, son," said Ernest Cargill, dishing out another sod of trifle.

"What's that, Mr Cargill?" Peggy asked.

"Ernest, Ernest. Everybody does. Everybody as nice as you."

Does he mean to insult her, Norman wondered, but his mother was moving around in her chair in a pleased way and he could tell her mind was not on his father's evening meal as it regularly was at this time.

"What do you need to be a piano tuner, Mr Cargill?" asked Norman.

"I should have thought you'd know that." Mr Cargill spoke in a dismissive voice. The change was as between an open and a closed door into a welcoming shop, overspilling bags and colour one moment, the bell and the shutters the next.

Peggy was quick to notice affront to her son and picked in her bag for her purse. Cargill saw that he had lost some purchase over her although he could not place the cause.

"Real solid-gold copper-bottomed talent. That's what you need. And I'll undertake that's what you've got." He stretched back on the wooden chair that was like a school chair, and rolled his body at Peggy and Norman. It was perfectly egg-shaped, the little shoulders giving onto a dome of stomach and curving down to the start of the insectlike legs, the long fly of the trousers threateningly flat.

For two weeks after that, Norman did not collect his mother after work. He had not yet met Denise, but he liked the piano tuner to whom he was apprenticed, and went back some evenings to have dinner with him and his wife. They had two rolls for the pianola that had been made from the actual playing of Rachmaninov.

"We've no pianola, maybe, but the potential to hear that great player himself. You can look at those holes and just tell. Hearing it might be a disappointment. The piano would not be anything like the one he played. This way though, I see the intervals," said the piano tuner. "That's how it is on paper. The holes don't hold like the notes you hear. There's a space around them."

Ernest Cargill began to call round at the haberdasher's.

He bought bits of ribbon and yards of elastic, explaining that these were for tying mirrors in the cages of his budgerigars and holding the night-cosies close around the cages. He did not say who sewed him the elasticated cosies, or if he made them himself. One day, he bought two and a half yards of fawn wool, and asked for it to be wrapped, together with as many balls of white angora as would make a short-sleeved jumper. The soft balls and the folded cloth were left at the door for Peggy that night as she left the shop, wrapped in stout brown paper and tied with the kind of string that is reluctant to repeat its knotting in reverse.

Since she was a good housewife, however, Norman's mother slowly unpicked the string. Stan watched, not interested but offended at this unusual turn to his evening. The room was as it had always been in Norman's life, a green kitchen up to waist height, cream up the rest of the walls, pipes under the sink coughing, the pulley of washing hauled up to the ceiling.

Peggy rolled the string into a tidy loop, waisted it with its end, and set it aside. She opened the parcel's brown paper like a book and lifted up the kittenish angora, ball after ball. Each one she carried to the work bag that hung off the back of the chair she used, and stowed it. She behaved as though she were being lent these balls of wool just to look after for a time, for someone else.

Stan said, "Does this mean I'm to starve?"

Peggy said, and Norman recognised that she was now able to give because she had been given to, "I'll do rich pastry with onion gravy over beef mince and the pie and cream to follow."

Then her son knew that she had not been buying the cream that had recently appeared in their lives.

His father, he saw, was directly pleased about the dinner to come, too tired to consider its actual source. His mother wrapped the skirt length up in the brown paper. She put it away with the winter blankets in the wooden box on the stair.

As he watched the angora jumper take shape between his mother's softly probing, softly conversing knitting needles, Norman saw the new way she would be seen by Mr Cargill take shape in the white wool. She would be a woman fed with cream and dressed in wool – fed and dressed by him. He wondered if she knew how plain a small eventual surrender appeared to her son, or if she knew of it herself.

His father continued apparently unaware. This pleased Norman, for he did not think that any surrender to Mr Cargill by his mother need be definitive. He could imagine her accepting something quite innocent in the way of an offer – a trip to the pictures, a walk – and how surprised she would be and bothered by the spelling out of the unsaid. At that stage, Norman believed, he could still stave off Mr Cargill, perhaps with some offputting filial behaviour. Then it would be only a matter of weeks until Mr Cargill became another of the quiet jokes linking mother and son in a way that did not prejudice the father but gave them patience with him.

Peggy and Mr Cargill married on Norman's twenty-eighth birthday. Although angora does not take dye and the jumper was not new, Peggy wore it, under a remodelled suit made of pre-war cloth. The furry wool over his mother's breast took Norman's attention. He thought of Mr Cargill's head there, the airy animality of the wool in his nostrils. He wondered whether it had been his mother's decision to wear the jumper, which might indicate an erotic bond between bride and groom, or Mr Cargill's, which would just go to show he was a mean old brute.

Peggy was fifty that year, her new husband – Ernest – sixty-eight years old.

"Lovely thing is, I'm retired. Or semi," Mr Cargill would say. "Semi meaning I still have to do as she says." At this he would indicate Peggy as though she had unfulfillable private whims.

Stan took it in silence. How it took him was in one fell swoop. From being a taciturn fit man in early middle age, he took on the manner and appearance of a broken grandfather. His pipe, which had been the fruity conclusion of each day, became his mouthpiece. He hid inside its smoke. Norman had the idea that once his father had sent out enough smoke he just absented himself, so that you might have been able to pass a hand clean through the wad of pipe smoke filling the kitchen chair on top of an old pair of corduroy legs. The beige tartan slippers that had only come out when Stan was ill were all he wore indoors now. He took to talking at night, outside, among the overblown cabbages and dithering moths. He would dig for hours, without energy or purpose, turning over the soil as though looking for something very small he had lost.

Stan's ears and cheeks grew whiskery, his veins purple. He ate little, removing his teeth for longer periods of time each day until he put them in only for visitors. His eyes hardened to a babyish unadapting blue. He seemed to be concentrating on missing all he could, as if the implications of anything might be too great to support. He felt the furniture as he progressed through his small house, touching it with hands that were always on the verge of trembling. The tone of the furniture in the house loosened. Two window sashes frayed away. The casement window in the eaves was opened minutely further each night by the ivy's furtive persistent growing.

Although Stan was ten years younger than Mr Cargill, it did not seem so in the first years of Peggy's new marriage. It was as though she had carried an indulgence from time away from the house where Norman grew up and into the detached brick house she now shared with Ernest Cargill. Norman feared that there was something in marriage – and by this time he *had* met Denise – that filled a man with a temporary defiance of time, a fullness as brute but as desirable as whatever it is that makes an apple an apple, a pear a pear. Norman too, never having experienced this fullness, began to fear its loss. Before sleep, he plotted its attainment.

Resistant to finding himself one day deserted or widowed, Norman at this time resisted marriage.

He was visiting his father, sanding the back of a rough-running drawer, when there was a knocking at the back door.

Stan pushed himself up out of his chair and moved towards the door, hollow-legged and slow, the slippers shuffling on the red oilcloth floor. The smoke sat where he had left it, over the chair.

It was Ernest Cargill, less weighty, less red, than he had looked before his marriage that had lifted time from him.

"Sit down," he said to Stan.

"It's my house," said Stan.

"You'll need to sit down."

"I know what I need."

"You'll need to get your father a hot drink," said his stepfather to Norman.

"It's his house," said Norman. There was a panting heart somewhere in the room, a hot unsaid phrase. As the youngest man of the three, linked through his mother to both the others, Norman listened to the silence and weighed it.

"Go on, Dad," he said, "sit down."

"That's right. That's it," said Ernest Cargill.

Norman looked at his stepfather, not a man to come to a back door, nor one to show consideration for his wife's first husband and his needs. All this talk of needing suggested that the chair, the hot drink were wanted to stem a need for more than merely rest or refreshment.

When he had the two stubbornly silent old men – for they seemed to have come closer in years by this contact with one another – sat down with cups of tea, Norman asked Mr Cargill:

"Was it fatal?"

He did not understand where this question had come from and worried as he spoke that he might not make himself clear.

"I mean to say: is my mother going to live? Or are we beyond that?"

Stan looked as though the idea of her death were not so far from the fact of her departure. He did not seem shaken, nor satisfied, but shrunk and cold. The latent trembling of his shiny-skinned hands ticked into action, that was all. He could only run down from here.

Mr Cargill stepped towards Stanley and shook him warmly by the beating hand, as though catching a bird.

"*You* will understand what a blow this is to me, Stan," he said. "Only you, very likely. Since it could have been you she was married to."

"It was," said Stan.

Norman made the second cups of tea he could see were in order.

Four years later, he was still making cups of tea for the two old men, washing, cooking and cleaning for them, collecting their bandages, powders and pills. For his father had been made old by the same clot in Peggy's brain that had widowed Mr Cargill when she fell down over the counter at the haberdashers, setting off a long hoop of curtain tape that bowled smoothly across the floor, havered and fell flat, dry as a spent coin.

It was not until he had nursed first his father and then the less destructible Mr Cargill until there was no more to be done that young Norman, born in 1921, was able to marry Denise and move into their first home together, the retirement apartment at the conjunction of one busy and one quiet road, where they lived with abandoned youthful carelessness within their love, even if it seemed to one passing that they were an old couple content to sit knitting and smoking under the gaze of a cat with a rhythmic tail and a clock that would not tell much more time.

A Tower of Silence

Nargis Walker

All of this was generating a type of heat which made her feel faint. It wasn't the first time that she had made this speech. She had practised it in her head until the words were perfect, polished pebbles of sound which glinted and skittered in the echoing recesses of her thoughts. She cleared her throat and spoke quietly, so that the small group of people looked up at her, focusing on her calm and resolute figure. Several of them were weeping. Her own eyes felt hot and dry as if in a fever.

"He was a good man. I say that, knowing full well that a good man is difficult to live with. Many of you have known him, us, since the earliest days of our relationship and some from way before then. For me, meeting him was a privilege and a deeply formative experience. I had known . . ."

There was a rude hammering on the door. "For God's sake Zenobia, are you going to be in there all night?" She sighed as she stood up in the bathtub, the heat steaming off her body in little crematorial puffs. For the moment, the obituary would have to wait. It was right and proper that she should rehearse it, of course, one never knew when one would need it. Doubtless she would have plenty of opportunity to revise the content over the years, that is if they were still together then and had not become part of the divorce statistics and assuming they were married first. How else could one make such a public announcement these days about love and such like without seeming mawkish? For the moment anyway, paragraphs two, three, four and five of the obituary were discreetly shrouded and removed so as not to cause offence.

The subject of the speech was waiting outside, looking astonishingly healthy and not a little irritated. A handsome face, with bones to die for (metaphorically speaking) and deep lines running into interesting furrows and dips.

"Come on, we'll be late," he said. She pointed two barrelled fingers at him.

"Bang, bang, you're dead," she said lightly, without the slightest trace of a smile.

So, what had her mother said to her down the telephone when she told them about him? It had hurt. There was no use pretending otherwise. A silly piece of nonsense, uttered by a sad lady with three dead children and a fourth about to marry a white man. Was this an excuse or was there any truth in what she had said? Of course not, it was a voice full of fears and disbelief that had said it.

"So, Zenobia, brown boys are not good enough for you?" She had been stunned into a silence which her mother had misread as proof of her words. No use protesting that the only other man she had considered marrying had actually been black. Not that that would have mattered, she would have been even more horrified by that. It was a precise shade of brown that she had been after, a paler shade of brown. In that moment, on either end of the telephone line hung equal weights of anger and displeasure, straining the bond which had only ever just about held them together. And yes, she was jealous of her brothers again, even the dead one. She was convinced her mother would have made an effort to understand if it had been one of them. But for her? No chance. She tried to keep her bitterness under control. Why give her the satisfaction of noting it? It never went, this jealousy, even though one of the recipients of the feeling was no longer alive. It simply pounded with an unabated rhythm as it had always done.

"For Christ's sake," she muttered, partly to herself. "You don't know what you're talking about."

"What did you say?" came the voice back sharply, a brief shard of razor line clarity on a wire crackling with dissonance, distress and disappointment.

"This is Bombay. Your three minutes are up. Do you require more time?"

"No . . . yes . . . Look, just get off the line please."

"No need for being rude, madam, just doing my job. Are you wanting another three minutes?"

"Yes, yes, sorry. We'll have more time please." A pause. Was it a pause? Then her mother's voice again.

"So, Zenobia, does this young man have a name?"

"Yes, sorry. Black actually, David Black." Damn, that was twice she had had to say sorry. It made her sound defensive.

"As in whisky, yes? Black and White," her mother said drily. "And so black is white." Had she said that last sentence or had Zenobia imagined it? Not like Mummee. Too clever by half and she couldn't credit her with that.

"Daddee kah che? Is he there? I need to speak to him. He'll understand." Another pause. Amusement. Then, very slowly, very deliberately:

"You think so? He sends his love. He sends his apologies. But he can't come to the phone. Your father is . . . not feeling too well. The wedding is in April you say? The first? Very appropriate. All Fools' day."

Zenobia was silenced. She chalked up another imaginary point to Mrs Rustomji. This was the most cutting speech her mother had ever made. It was so unlike her. "So . . . clever," she thought lamely. Her mother was winning this conversation on points by an alarming margin. And she wasn't clever. Or sharp. Not her mother. She was the complete "wife", the complete "mother". Eternal, always there in sickness and in health, invisible, a prop, a mat, a backdrop against which anyone could shine. And each adjective with which she labelled her mother was instantly dipped in vitriol and polished to a sheen with dismissal.

But her mother had come to the wedding. And she had smiled. And she had pleaded a hundred times before the event. "Nini, darling, do you really want this? You know this is a big step?"

"Mummee, chup, shut up. Do you really think I haven't thought about this? Yes of course I really want this. And please stop calling me by that absurd name."

Her mother had sighed loudly. She had capitulated, she had accepted everything. She had never used the name again. Zenobia had taken it all for granted. It was, after all, her mother who needed to change.

A year is a long time in a marriage, each extra year a gift shared between equals. But when mothers and daughters learn and share each other's deepest secrets, when they acknowledge each other's pain, there is a drawing back of the umbilical cord, turning ever inwards and winding closer, until wound about with the silk of their sharings they are bound together again in the most intimate of space. And then time, any time is too short. It vanishes like the hint of a bird's breath on a frosty morning.

And so it was for Zenobia.

The sheets of rain had fallen relentlessly outside. The balcony, a delight of bougainvillaea and jasmine and tubs of glistening marigolds on a sunny day, looked drab and sodden, the tiles stained with the dust and dirt that hung like opaque glass between the city and the sun, swept earthwards by the force of the rain. Mr Rustomji had assured his daughter and the new Angrezi son-in-law that the difference between Indian weather and the English summer was that in England the weather was unpredictable. Whereas, in

India, it would rain heavily as if on cue every morning of the monsoon and then, with the earth refreshed, the rain would give way to a fine clear evening. With a certain ironic disregard, the rain had subsequently rained without stop for three weeks. Even the Blacks' two weeks travelling up North, courtesy of the Rustomjis, had been marred by grey skies. Now back in the flat, the sense of claustrophobia was mounting. It carried with it a deep foreboding which made no sense. Everyone was on their best behaviour.

It was understood, that as a white man with an underdeveloped immunity to the various germs at large in Bombay, David Black was going to have to be protected constantly. Everyone was solicitous that his food and drink should come only from the most guarded of sources: food cooked in the home, water boiled so ferociously that no microorganism could possibly survive. Only it was Zenobia who succumbed, and for ten whole days she developed an intimate knowledge of the inside of the toilet bowl. Each time she emptied her retching guts, her mother held her hand, her forehead, and when each bout ended, her head lolled on Mrs Rustomji's bosom, grateful for the softness, the reassurance, the sweetness of her breath lifting the sour fumes rising from her own body. She felt afraid. Perhaps she was dying. The unmistakable smell of death seemed to follow her everywhere.

It was as if the physical contact forged a close empathy, so that, slowly, mother and daughter made their first tentative attempts to communicate. There was a simultaneous cessation of hostilities, and an end to the petty conversations which said little of any consequence. Their new awareness of each other was a fragile lace of emotions, a perilous structure of words that threatened to blow over at the slightest inclemency. Mrs Rustomji remarked gently, by way of a bouquet proffered with sincerity, that she was amazed how well David could chop onions.

"A very nice boy, Zenobia, so nice in every way. Only . . ." her voice hovered wistfully, "he's not a Parsi." Zenobia nodded in acknowledgement. A year into her marriage, she was grateful for her parents' understanding and compassion. She had heard the uncles had suggested disowning her for her disgraceful behaviour. One of them had confided shamefacedly to Zenobia that her mother had been very dignified. "Masa," she had said, "I have lost enough children already. Why should I lose my only daughter too?"

"Zenobia," the uncle had said, "your mother is a too good woman."

Zenobia was inclined to agree. In the next three weeks, they unpicked between them the barriers of a lifetime, stick by stick, stone by stone. Sometimes they did this quickly and feverishly, sometimes with looks and few words. The long shadows of her brothers receded. They told each other things from the past, the same stories that each of them knew, but with new twists so that with the flick of a sentence from one to the other, a new understanding unfolded, a reversible fabric woven from a shared past but viewed now on one side, now the other. And Zenobia discovered for the first time a shy, sensitive but enormously strong woman. She had sought feminist heroines in a thousand different places, in fact and in fiction, role models to admire and emulate. Dolt that she was, she had never recognised this mild-mannered heroine. She could not have described her mother as feminist, nor would the term have been one her mother would have recognised. She had not been one to blaze trails for the advancement of her sex, but in her own way, she was a woman to admire, the shiny rust-proof backbone of her family. Zenobia hoped that her mother could actually begin to like her, for she never doubted that she loved her. Now, belatedly, she herself was stricken with love for her mother.

And the days ticked by irrevocably. There were only a few days left before the Blacks were to return to England.

Zenobia was filled with a sadness she could not dispel. She told herself that it was only a matter of months before her parents would visit again in the late spring. The two of them would be together again, they would be able to fill the days with talks and hugs. She would have children too, so her mother could play with them and overfeed them and spoil them.

Two days before they leave, the rain stops. David Black has had enough of the rain; the melancholy that lurks in the corners of the flat; the incessant heat that pours down on them; the fluttering of wings as flies beat against the glass and the mosquitoes scream their terrorist attacks on every exposed part of his body. They go downstairs to catch one of the little black and yellow Bombay cabs to the cinema. Out of the flat, an upstairs/downstairs house man himself, he feels liberated. As they wave at the first taxi, the driver peers at them through the glass, shakes his head, swears. The second one stops but someone else pushes past them, slamming the door in their faces. No more taxis to be seen. His wife goes back upstairs, perhaps they could cadge a lift with his father-in-law.

In the flat, as the door opens, Mrs Rustomji stands silhouetted against the wall, hand pressed to her chest, pink sari billowing as the door opens to her daughter. She tries to smile.

They never get to the cinema that evening. Zenobia sits with her mother on the back verandah, staring out at the stars, Mrs Rustomji's eyes unseeing in the dark.

"Zenobia, jaan, I feel scared," she whispers.

In another room, David Black finally succumbs to Bombay, his guts and bowels in revolt. Zenobia holds her mother's hand, flitting backwards and forwards between mother and husband. It occurs to her that she and her mother are exchanging roles and she plays mother, the homebody, all concern for her family. And the weight of the role is enormous, crushing. Finally, Mrs Rustomji pats her hand. "You must sit with your husband, goodnight jaan." Mr Rustomji fusses his wife to bed.

It is a steaming hot night and the fan in the Blacks' room barely stirs the tired air as it churns and turns. Outside the dogs howl for the souls of the dead. Explosions fill the night air. David Black groans in his sleep. And Zenobia, tossing in a fitful dream between waking and sleep, can no longer tell what is real and what springs from her nightmares. The doorbell rings and Zenobia flings herself out of bed. The smell of death is now so close she can feel the mortuary chill through the heat. She scuttles to join her father who is shutting the front door. The clock on the wall says 3.00 a.m.

"Who was it?" she whispers.

"A telegram to say Alanmai in Navsari has died, poor woman, may her soul rest in peace."

The chill of death recedes. It is for someone else.

"Daddee, what are the explosions? And why are the dogs howling? Bapaiji used to say that's when they smell death." She is suddenly reduced to a whimpering child. Her father smiles in the gloom.

"This is Bombay not Bexley. Those are firecrackers for some Hindu festival. And the dogs always bark, it's all the noise. Anyway, I thought you Western types didn't believe in that sort of thing." He chuckles and shakes his head gently. "Now go back to sleep or we'll wake Mummee."

An hour later, she is in an uneasy sleep. A single screaming howl from a dog pierces her sleep. Her father is knocking gently but insistently on the door.

"Zenobia," he calls urgently, "Mummee has died." Just that. He stands there in his pyjamas and bare feet, looking bewildered.

Now the howl rises from deep inside her.

When the white van comes to take her mother, the house is heaving with relatives. An aunt is full of admiration for David. "Look at that," she sighs, "making cups of tea for everyone, our men would never be able to do that."

Zenobia sits mesmerised by her mother's bedside long after the body has gone. Once again there is a silence between her and her mother. On the pillow, a dark, vital, springy hair which she lifts gingerly between finger and thumb. It curls in her hands like a query. A picture of disbelief.

For the first time, Zenobia was driven through the gates. Her mother had always protected her from this before. The Towers of Silence. How often had her mother been through these gates before? She had been there to pray over her father, his bones broken in a billion places from the cancer. Then six months later, for her mother, just days before the birth of her best-beloved son. Then for her mother-in-law, her own two babies. Then only eighteen months ago, in an agony of grief for her best-beloved son. And now here was Zenobia, come to pray for her.

The sun broke through the clouds but the drive up the hill was through thick, lush vegetation that filtered it out. Peacocks strutted like Death's whores, their melancholy calls resounding to beguile the souls of the dead. In the small grey building, in the women's enclosure, the aunts and the shock of her mother's naked body laid on the stone slab waited for her.

"We have to bathe her and pray, make her ready for the journey. You must help us clean her."

That once so soft flesh, hard and cold. The hair curling, steely grey over the sweep of her forehead. Everything seen through a mist.

The time of prayer, the sandalwood burning, the fruit and offerings to please the wandering soul on its way to rest.

The white-face priests, and then the pall-bearers, those whey-faced men set apart from the rest of the community with sunken eyes and claw-like hands. She cried out as they lifted her mother to take her to the towers, the wells. She who had so loved her food, was to be made the feeding. Overhead, the vultures were already circling in anticipation.

She argued then with the two French tourists who had wandered in, wanting photographs of the towers and the mourners. It was sacred ground, they had no right to be there, it was forbidden. But all she could remember was "C'est pas possible," in the face of their hostility and intrusive curiosity. The tears and the anger distorting her face.

In the flat, David Black, excluded because he was not a Parsi, lay on his bed and heard the voice of Mrs Rustomji, calling for her husband. For Zenobia, there was only the silence.

The Sign

Ann Gilchrist

Greta first flew the night the sorcerer came. People were whispering, "The witch has been through the village, there's the sign." They held off. Greta picked it up, a smooth oval disc, ebony and bone, hanging from a stretched greasy leather string. It looked bigger than it felt in her hand. Perhaps that was because of the magic. There was a message on the sign, cut into the surface. She could feel it with her forefinger and thumb. Villagers watched. A youth of her own age with a puckered scar on his right cheek watched closest of all. She swung the disc on its thong and notes of light reverberated from it, tiny shards of gold from the edge of the disc flashing across the faces of the watchers. They shuffled back, the young man moved towards her. He wore mismatched rubber flip-flops, one blue, one red, and his denim trousers were held up with a worn fabric belt. He held out his hand, palm up, for the witch's gift. Greta shook her head. The sign was heavy and hot in the hollow of her hand and she knew that the witch had left it for her. The youth turned away and melted into the crowd.

Where she lived on the edge of the African Lake, news seeped through the village like liquid spilt on earth. She ran the length of the main street, puffs of dry-season dust swirling around her bare feet, but her grandmother already knew of the witch's visit and the charm with the runes, by the time she came between the banana trees framing the opening into the courtyard.

Her home was a house of women. There was her mother whose job in the Mission Hospital helped to pay for the things they could not grow, batteries for the radio, and lengths of coloured cloth to make into dresses. Her grandmother was the village wise woman, story teller and, some said, shapeshifter. Greta had two older sisters but now they were married and lived in their husband's houses, growing food, keeping chickens, milking goats and bearing plump children. Of her dead father she knew little except that the Sky God had taken him in a thunderstorm as he fished for tilapia in the brown lake shrouded by blue water hyacinth.

Her grandmother, Bibi, was sitting now in the shadow of the overhanging iron roof, her bony legs and huge worn feet sticking straight out in front of her as she wove a mat. Her fingers, gnarled from years of hoeing the ground to grow cassava and sweet potato, mechanically plaited the strips of straw and ribbons of red plastic. She looked up as Greta came into the yard and held out her honey-coloured palm, as the young man in the crowd had done.

"Let me see."

Greta had never questioned her grandmother's authority in all her fifteen years – until now. She shook her head, but Bibi's ashy red-rimmed eyes looked at her and her arm was drawn out, her fingers uncurling to expose the black and ivory disc with its edging of light, lying in her hand. Reluctantly she gave it to her. Bibi weighed it in each hand, then swung it on the thin strip of leather.

"Yes," she said, "it has power." She closed her eyes and her voice grew firmer. "It has strong power."

A shiver ran down Greta's back.

"What do you mean Bibi? What do the marks say?"

Bibi's eyes remained shut and her voice was still the firmly pitched one she used when she dispensed potions and advice to the people of the village.

"It's meant for you, and it's for you to find its meaning."

Bibi opened her eyes, her voice was cracked and elderly again.

"Now, girl, where you been? Go get water, there's only drops left in the jar."

She handed the pendant back to Greta and fumbled at the waist of the layers of orange and scarlet shawls swathing her body to draw out a fine gold chain, the tiny links glimmering with the same sparks of yellow light that came from the disc.

"Wear it on this, and go get the water before your mama gets back and finds you idle."

Greta took the chain, threaded it through the hole at the tip of the charm and fastened it round her neck. Then she picked up the big red plastic bucket and sauntered off towards the water pump at the edge of the market place.

The market was closing for the day but head-shaved, earlobe-dangling mamas were still selling piles of tomatoes, dried beans measured out in Blue Band tins from pyramids piled on newspaper, and bottles of brown liquid for malaria, easy childbirth and snakebite. Greta acknowledged their greetings but did not stop to talk. Her mother said she was bird-boned, bird-brained and bird-tongued but really it was just that she liked the thoughts in her own head best.

Under the mango tree, boys were cutting discarded lorry tyres into shapes and strips to make sandals. Beer-bellied men drank from scuffed brown bottles and, guffawing, told one another dirty stories and discussed cattle and bride prices.

They made suggestive remarks as Greta passed but she ignored them. Ever since her body had filled with puberty and her breasts budded and flourished she had had to listen to these men and the words that millet beer put into their mouths. Only her position as Bibi's granddaughter protected her from some of the things she knew the other girls in the village had to put up with. For here, in this country, where the majority lived in poverty, most men were denied power, except over women.

A young man moved away from the group of sandal

makers and came towards her. It was the same young man who had asked for the witch's sign, earlier in the day. He was tall and his skin bloomed like a ripe aubergine. When he grinned at her his scar disappeared into the folds of his smile. His name was Simba, "like the lion," he said and threw back his head letting the most amazing roar come from his mouth. Greta laughed.

As they walked to the well he told her that he had come to live with his uncle in the village, to find work. His home was in the hills to the south where there had been little rain for many years and the earth could not grow enough to support all those who lived there. Greta listened. The disc on the chain tickled her breastbone as he talked.

That night Greta slept on the wooden bed in the mud and cement brick house where she had been born and lived all her life. On the ceiling boards above her, bats and lizards pirouetted, the rhythm of their feet like the clacking of the mango-stone anklets worn by the snake dancers who visited the village. She held the witch's sign, warm and glittering, as she slept, and magic and reason mingled.

Then Greta flew. She woke up and felt the nubs of wings sprouting like rice shoots from her shoulder blades. At first they were just fluffy bumps but when she sat up in bed they grew faster. By the time she pushed aside the leather curtain at the opening to the house they were fully formed.

She flew as if she were a marsh owl, across ground, dried and creased as a paper bag, where fire-coloured dust sparkled in the indigo twilight. As the night grew darker she could see the flicker of kerosene lamps, like sequins dropped on the rusty red earth. She flew across the village. People looked up and saw only a paradise flycatcher. By the ice-blue flame of the moon she saw Simba sitting beneath a frangipani tree. She landed beside him so quietly that he did not hear her arrive and started when he turned. He did not notice the white wings folded down the pebbles of her spine but smiled and held her hand, then touched her blossoming breasts and toffee-tipped nipples.

Fire rippled through her bones and shivers ran across her belly and thighs as if a nest of tiny mice wriggled and danced behind her pubic bone. He smelt of cloves and cinnamon and told her she tasted of honey and papaya. When the membrane signifying her virginity tore as he entered her there was a sharp pain but then it was like sucking sugar cane, the taste buds in her body tingling, sweet and sharp at the same time. When the splashy dawn broke she flew home holding the charm and knowing that a spell had been cast or broken, she wasn't sure which.

The next night and for many nights afterwards, Greta went to bed holding the disc between her fingers. When the sky was dark violet she left her bed, felt her wings flower and flew to Simba where they enjoyed one another's bodies as men and women do. No turning back now.

Greta became pregnant. Bibi recognised the signs almost as soon as she did. In this place where men regarded women as their property and women's bodies were for use by men, there was little disgrace in not having a husband and no judging of Greta's swollen belly and breasts. Simba refused to acknowledge the child was his. He told people that the only woman who had shared his bed had come to him in the night as a purple-breasted bee eater or a Nubian nightjar, but when the early morning sun rose, it was always a bird that flew from his bed, not Greta.

The village began to talk. They remembered the day the witch had dropped the sign in the main street and they whispered again behind their hands that Greta's grandmother was a shapeshifter. Simba disappeared. Back to his home in the south, some said. To the big town on the other side of the Lake to look for work, said others.

Greta was troubled. In hurt and confusion, she cried. She still had the charm, but she no longer flew. How could she soar through the sky while her body tethered her to the earth as surely as if she were a goat on the end of a length of hemp? And she continued to swell, till her bird-boned frame could hardly hold upright, so pulled was it by the weight of the child inside her. And people continued to gossip and the men under the mango tree were no longer constrained by the knowledge that she was Bibi's granddaughter. Their remarks carried clearly to her as she walked past, the heavy red bucket on her head.

When her waters broke and the contractions began, Bibi was with her and her mother stayed home from work for the birth. Greta was in labour for a whole day and most of the next night. As the pain rose and fell she held the sign and heard Mama and Bibi discussing whether they should take her to the Mission Hospital. Before they could decide there was an enormous pressure inside her and finally something broke free from the imprisoning circle of her body. She felt a moment of relief and peace before Mama screamed and Bibi broke into a long keening wail. Greta caught a glimpse of dark skin, cat-like fur and feathers drenched in blood before Bibi snatched the thing and rushed out of the hut. She could hear a crunching sound and a growling screech. There was a smell of cinnamon, honey and kerosene as Bibi threw something onto the embers of the fire. Sour smoke swirled through the cracks in the hut wall making Greta and her mother cough and choke.

The day after the birth, Greta left her home. Her body was still bruised and bleeding as she walked towards the Lake. Standing at the edge, soft squelchy mud oozed between her toes. She swung her arm back and hurled the witch's sign as hard and as far as she could across the surface, pitted with islands of hyacinth. There was a slither of silence as a shadow crossed the water, then a greedy gulping as the Lake swallowed the disc. She turned and walked along the baked earth road that led away from the village.

The Cheated Eye

Catherine Eisner

Of course, her first emotion, when she learned her husband was living with his Russian interpreter, was utter relief. No longer was he to be found brooding in his garden room, amber decanter glinting by his side, wearing that wintry smile whenever their eyes met.

Then new feelings of resentment seized her. Looking from her study window to his room below, she could see, under the lattice of the glass roof, her husband's whorled crown of dark shaggy hair – thinning in the centre, she noticed – where he had slumped forward, beard on chest, feigning sleep. Playing possum was invariably his ruse when unwelcome questions remained unanswered. And those he had answered had been matters-of-fact, cursorily conveyed with his face turned from her.

He had said no more than that he was living in his unleased town flat with a young woman named Nadezhda. He called her Nadia, a Russian from Saratov who had never visited the West before. He said she was unworldly, and in the city she was endangered by a childlike inexperience. At heart, he said, she was an unsophisticated, provincial girl who was prey to primitive superstitions. Without too much thought he had bestowed on her his protection.

"All that you imagine is probably true," Leon had said. Beyond that he would say nothing more.

She slammed the window and saw his eyelids flicker. So be it, she decided, if he chose to retreat behind a carapace of calculated indifference, then she would contrive her manner to be no different from his – yet, she vowed, before the week was ended it was her intention to unbeard a lifetime of manifold deceptions.

First Report – "The Stakeout"

The next day she obeyed her new resolution by seating herself at the street frontage of a Greek café opposite the city mansion block where, behind the pane of a first floor window, could just be glimpsed the tip of a dismantled "To Let" sign – a visible token of the collapse of any pressing interest Leon might have had in selling the lease.

She had rejected the *baklava* and had been drinking slowly from a single glass of bitter tea for over an hour, watching the lemon slice sink as the sun westered behind the roofs, when she saw a young woman mount the steps and pause outside the apartments' entrance.

Nadia. Unquestionably. A tall, slender, doleful girl with wispy, duckpond-brown hair, very short skirt, early twenties, wearing, she was certain, Leon's newest black leather zipped jerkin.

The girl with the duckpond-brown hair unlocked the door and entered. Within a few moments a light was switched on in Leon's flat and Nadia, if indeed the shadowy form was hers, appeared at the window staring down at the street and the square beyond.

The café had emptied. (*Establishing shot, exterior, day,* she thought, *location: Moscow Road leading to St Petersburgh Place, London* W2. She jotted a note on the last pages of her "Activities Report". *Time: 17.30 hours. Shadows long.*) She rose to leave. The sign above her read: *Thank You For Not Smoking* PIPE *or* CIGAR *when café doors are closed.*

As she walked to Bayswater Station (*tracking shot*), she marshalled on her fingers her next manoeuvres. [i] The over-ruling strategem was to gain entry to the flat. (She had lived in the flat with Leon practically all their married life, but, when they had moved permanently to their pied-à-terre cottage, she was certain *her* keys had been sent to the estate agent; a request for them now would be bound to alert her husband.) [ii] The problem of temporary leave from her work must be overcome – she would need many spare hours for surveillance. [iii] She must make certain Leon had no hint of her actions.

Her last thought was jolted by the sudden emergence of Leon crossing the station concourse towards her. Mercifully undetected, she ducked out of sight beside a kiosk and observed her husband hasten by, his eyes set on a more distant quarry. His long hair blew in tufts, a moving plant. (*Fadeout.*)

The keys

(*Flash forward*). That evening, she again reviewed the obstacles. Unless she could recover the flat's keys – covertly – she was lost. The telephone rang. Leon.

When she said, "Why don't you hang up?" Leon said, "Where's the difference, you're hung up, whatever," and slammed down the receiver.

And then, reluctantly – had Leon's words goaded her? – she remembered the plastic holdall on the top shelf of the hall closet. Memories surfaced and resubmerged. The lightning darts of her mind were like so much cross-hatching that had begun to etch a picture of her predicament, until she saw, as yet indistinct, the semblance of the path she should take.

(*Cutaway. Over-the-shoulder shot.*) Mounted on a pair of steps, she withdrew the holdall from where it had lain, unopened, for more than five years. (*Reverse angle view.*) She bit her lip, tears brimming. She felt as weak as water.

(*Cue closeup.*) Holdall.

(*Medium shot.*) In her bedroom, door locked – yet there was no other in the cottage except her small dog – she hesitantly unzipped the holdall and tipped the contents onto her bed.

Item 1. Two latchkeys with sticking plaster labels bearing her own name – *Miriam.* (So it was as she suspected, Aunt Wilma *had* kept their flat's keys – entrusted to her more than fifteen years before. Leon would certainly have forgotten.)

Item 2. A military flashlight. (Her mouth dried. An uneasy memory stirred; swiftly suppressed.)

Item 3. A soiled surgical corset, the elasticated panels begrimed and buffed glossy with human spoil. (She was riven by a prolonged shudder and fell to her knees beside the bed.)

Item 4. A baby's pink crocheted woollen blanket, frayed at its edges, with an embroidered initial *M.* As she fingered the soft, familiar fabric – smelled its sour lactic traces – her heart broke and she wept. (*Wipe.*)

Second Report – "Childes Mass"

At first light, Miriam crossed the allotments to the schoolyard. Her little white dog trotted behind her. She noticed the sky was in the likeness of blown glass cooling; soon the horizon would be entirely clear.

She descended into the crypt and entered the classrooms – a giant striding among the child-sized furniture. She made sure all the sensorial materials and equipment for her exploration classes – the activity trays, the wooden blocks and plastic containers – were correctly arranged in their places along the wall. From above she heard the nuns at their matins.

As the strains of the harmonium and their earnest voices reached her, she was drawn to the entrance porch, hands exploring the dusty ledge immediately below the warm air duct. She pulled down the flaps of a cardboard box to stroke the bedraggled feathers of the injured starling Andrea had rescued. The youngest in her class, the boy alone was charged with the duty to feed the foundling. A glass pipette for the purpose lay in the straw. Andrea was just five years old yet appeared younger. His lustrous black hair was brilliantined and smelled of oil of roses. He was astigmatic, viewing his world through spectacles fitted with a frosted lens. He taunted the other children to attract their scorn, which once gained, reduced him to tears. He wore a black armband.

In the front of her "Activities Report" Miriam had jotted, "Mother dcd. No siblings. V. critical to orient A towards self-reliance through personal work-cycle to gn snse scl rspnsblty."

Under her hand the bird protested feebly, emitting a mournful "Krrrr," then, wing drooping, rolling with a bandy-legged gait, teetered away from her grasp. The smudged feathers, she noted, reminded her of foxed crepe.

(*Dissolve.*)

(The Sister Directress looked searchingly into Miriam's eyes when the subject of leave was broached. But she agreed willingly enough to a proposal of staggered time blocks to suit Miriam's absences. They had known each other since Miriam's early days as a film student. An ardent admirer of *Potemkin*, Miriam had chosen to film a homage to Eisenstein's erratic staccato style at this very school. The result was *Childes Mass* – a 16mm B/W single-reeler of bleached fades and clumsy defocused transitions with rapid heteroclite jump-cut frames that documented the playgrounds of an urban childhood. In the end, despite an Hons, Miriam was irresistibly drawn to the wisdom of the Sisters' teaching traditions, and had remained at the school – a convert of a kind – like a genre painter who saw no reason to stray from her first subject.)

Third Report – "Componential Analysis"

Miriam unlocked the door to the familiar vestibule. She sniffed and recognised the brand of floor polish that Mrs Bryce used for the tiled landings.

As she mounted the lower treads, she heard the first floor flat door open and voices rebounded in the stairwell. (*Ambient sound: footsteps, exterior traffic movement.*)

She retreated into the shadowy recess beneath the stairs. (*Canted dutch angle shot with limbo lighting.*) Her husband descended with Nadia in tow. (*Continuity note*: Leon wears a dark suit, black shirt, no tie; Nadia wears forest-green nylon parka with jersey shirt of matching colour and tan chinos.)

Crossing the lobby, Miriam's husband laid his hand on Nadia's shoulder and gave a coarse laugh.

"In the right hands it could be hilarious," Leon said, and snickered once more.

Nadia disengaged his hand as she opened the door.

"Tell me, *Lvyonok*," said Nadia, inconsequentially, pronouncing the words thickened, as though her teeth were grinding on ice, "who is that *Amerikanetz* whose name sounds like a sneeze?" They closed the outside door before Miriam heard Leon's answer.

(*Boom crane shot.*) Inside the flat, from the street window, she watched them depart towards Bayswater. She switched on the tape deck of Leon's recording console. (*Indo-Jazz Fusions* by Joe Harriet and John Mayer.) She felt another wound opening; she had an image of a third tongue savouring their shared pleasures.

In the bedroom she slid open the fitted wardrobe. She examined the labels of Leon's new clothes. A Zegna silk tie. A zipped leather blouson by Cerrutti (his *studied* jacket, he had joked) and a pure cashmere overcoat by Brioni from Beal & Inman, both black. Plainly, Leon's arduous three-month assignment in Russia, constructing colossal sets for the 2nd Unit of a pan-European actioneer, had not been without its consolations – or without its *trophies*. She recoiled at the hateful sound of a scented silk slip slithering from a hanger.

But Leon's nature she knew – intimately. It was the hidden dossier that recorded the lineaments of Nadia's desires that she had entered this room to read; to turn each page of her Russian soul. She smelled the pillow then tracked Nadia's perfume to its source – a philtre of *Krasnaya Moskva* in the bathroom cabinet. She stood by the unmade bed, turned to the penultimate page of her "Activities Report", and began to write:

1) *Note on bed to Leon*: "Lover-Lyova-Lyovka! Remember collect eggs, saffron and fizzy candles you promised. And Lyovushka! All must chill until tomorrow. Wait! Be tempted not! Yr N." (In the kitchen, Miriam opened the fridge to find it crammed with covered glass dishes of vivid, exquisitely prepared *zakuski* and a towering *charlotte russe*.) (*Freeze frame.*) She scowled. A pang of childish envy. A celebration? But of what? On the fridge door was taped a picture postcard from Bournemouth. She turned one corner to read the message in a familiar scrawl.
2) *Postcard*: "Still soaking up the photons. L. L." (*Love Laurence* . . . Leon's best friend was a confirmed bachelor and xenophobe and would not have dreamt of holidaying anywhere but on the south coast. He was a linguistics specialist – a pedant, but a passionate one. Once, he had attempted to explain to Miriam his theory of ambiguity in contextually-sensitive componential analysis, but when she had stifled a yawn he had given up.)
3) *Icon of St Nadezhda* (devotional print mounted on card above bd) & stub of burnt candle in cndlhldr in frame.
4) *Extract*: Paperback copy of Mikhail Bulgakov's *The Master and Margarita*, with passage from Chapter 13 on page 149 marked in yellow fluorescent highlighter pencil. (*N.B.* Book on table on Leon's side of bed, but flyleaf inscribed *Nadezhda Stepanovna Cheremisovna*. *N.B.* Xanthichromatic quotation beginning: "Here his

eyes opened wide and as he whispered he gazed at the moon.")

5) *Textbooks*: Copies of *Learn to Interpret by Interpreting* by G. G. Yudina, Москва, and *Grammaire de la Langue Russe* by André Mazo, Institut d'Études Slaves, Paris (with dedication penned on title page: '. . . *ma nouvelle camarade d'armes adorée – aujourd'hui nous avons trouvé les mots. . . et il y a tant à dire et tant de lendemains!*')
6) *Draft letter from Benedict* (Leon's solicitor) to the Home Office applying for a "special extension to Miss Cheremisovna's work-permit" due to her "indispensable services" which were "essential to a major motion picture's successful post-production." (Miriam silently pledged never to have dealings with Benedict ever again.)
7) *Pocket English Grammar* edited by Laurence and dedicated to Leon. (At her wedding, she was sure the entire congregation must have known, except for Laurence perhaps, that Leon's best man had long carried a torch – as a flame is attracted to a brilliant, self-applauding butterfly – for the shockhaired bridegroom at her side. When Laurence's *Grammar* was at last published, Miriam believed that she, alone, understood that much of the text was a kind of *roman à clef* to be decrypted by no one but Laurence and herself. She flipped to page 237 of **Adverbial Clauses** and read, "Joyce wandered in, **the way that she does**," and **Modal Verbs**, page 47, "Leonard **must think** about the consequences of his actions." (Then there was a catch in her throat.) "**Since Joyce's father died**, she has not been able to sleep." And "Joyce" reappeared on page 233 under **Joining Clauses** as "Joyce is **either** *desperate*, **or** *just silly*" and, again, under **Possessive Pronouns** on page 187, "Leonard's wife is so beastly I think they must have bathroom towels labelled **his** and **its**." Joyce had been Miriam's maiden name.)

She closed her "Activities Report". Upon such slender data she was now confident she could conduct a bloody but decisive campaign.

The Glove

The doors to the Reading Rooms were still open when Miriam arrived an hour later. As she approached the portico, she hesitated to enter. Beside the door squatted one of the city's pavement bedouins, huddled with his traps under a filthy military tarpaulin. The upturned collar of the waterproof concealed the lower face but deep-set eyes swivelled after her, eloquent with reproach. On the ridge of the dado above his head an abandoned elbow-length silk evening glove (heraldically *appaumé*) pointed (*sinister*) to the hunched figure below.

Steeling herself, she crossed the threshold, rejecting the silent appeal. (Leon, one year shortly after they were married, when blessed with abundance, had invested in the entire print sequence of *Ein Handschuh*, a cycle of 10 etchings by the symbolist, Max Klinger.

"To look back," she mused, "and see ourselves good-looking," for the characteristics of Klinger's discarded glove as erotic fetish had not escaped her; her mouth lifted in her defining smile, her eyes somnolent yet watchful as a cat's, "when we would forget the days and think only of the nights."

Again her secret smile – pondering the futility – the folly – of attempting to revive past happinesses – and the lines composed themselves . . .

They had always found the equation yield.
Nightly, a certain figure over
the denominator gave the proof.
Now it's impossible to believe they held
that there was ever
an alchemy that could equal love.

The Reference Annex shut at half past four and already the keeper was cranking closed the fanlights beneath the cupola.

In her "Activities Report", under the heading of *Russian metanlität*, Miriam wrote, *Izlivat dushu* – "pouring out of the soul; the mingling of two lovers' souls, for example"; *Stradanyie* – "mental suffering due to unrequited love or coarseness of lover or spouse"; *Toska* – "melancholy homesickness"; *Grekh* – "a sense of sin only removed when sinner reaches a state of highly emotional repentance"; and, finally, *Tyomniye sili* – "dark or sinister, evil forces"; the latter she thrice underlined.

Fourth Report – "Dead Letter Box"

The following morning – a Wednesday – Miriam resumed sentry-go at the Greek café. She had skipped breakfast so she felt no sense of *Grekh* when she chose the *Siami* honeycake and ordered a cappuccino. Beside her, on a plinth, a bust of Hippocrates counted each calorie.

(*Available light.*) Across the street, Nadia emerged alone, with Leon's leather Cerruti slung over her shoulder. The girl narrowed her eyes against the harsh sunlight and sauntered off towards St Petersburgh Place.

(*Long take.*) The two women, ten paces apart, traversed the Park towards Kensington Gore. Laurence's "photons" danced between the leaves of the sycamores and winged seedpods spiralled down to meet the paving. There had been heavy rainfall in the night and pink worms had been flushed out of the grass and lay wriggling on the drying paths.

Miriam tasted sickness in the back of her throat. The sun scorched her shoulders and she removed her jacket . . .

So hot
the bench
in the park

carries its shadow
draped over
one arm

(*Closeup.*) A brilliant green leaf caterpillar landed on Miriam's breastbone where it remained, a bright enamelled emerald clasp.

Behind her, out of sight, Miriam heard a childish treble shout, "Nat! Donchawannatunabagel?" and she knew, with absolute certainty, that if she turned around, she'd see a small schoolboy on whose dark head of hair, attached by a hairgrip, would be a *yarmulke*. She turned. A small boy, wearing a red blazer, ran past in the heat haze. Perched on the back of his head was a skullcap. ("All that you imagine is probably true," Leon had said, yet, if Laurence's context-sensitive theory was to be believed, in a blind test no ambiguity concerning the derivational history of the boy's utterance could be admitted.)

Nadia paced across Rotten Row, her shoes making clear impressions in the dampened sandy gallops.

Miriam carefully trod in each of Nadia's footmarks – a sequence of steps that, with practice, she believed she could learn.

(*Rapid clips.*) A soldier cantered by, his horse kicking up a delighted pair of heels, obliterating Nadia's tracks.

(*Master shot. Church Square. Exterior. Day.*) After Nadia had produced a headscarf and entered the church, Miriam examined the noticeboard, squinting, as the sun bounced off the verdigris of the copper canopy. For several moments she remained puzzled by the Cyrillic characters and the Julian Calendar dates – then she fathomed that some two weeks separated the Old Style and New Style entries. By counting the days backwards she realised that this morning – at this precise moment – a 10.30 a.m. liturgy for St Nadezhda was being observed within.

(The saffron, Miriam suddenly surmised, was for Nadia's cake. A cake to celebrate the feast of her saint's day.)

(*Interior.*) Choral singing. Votive candles shone through the incense billows. Miriam choked on the fierce acridness, took two paces forward and entered Holy Mother Russia. Instinctively, she sought the concealment of a stone pillar. *Cut to* . . . The archpriest's hairy eyebrows like an imperial spreadeagle. *Cut to* . . . Nadia threading a path through the worshippers, approaching before the iconostasis to genuflect, bowing low, the heel of her right hand pressed against the floor. *Cut to* . . . Nadia rising to kiss the censed icon in front of the screen – first the hem of the Virgin, then the holy robe of the Infant. *Cut to* . . . Sparkle of candlelight as a tear (*Toska?*) brims and trickles down Nadia's jaw. She sniffs, and wipes her cheek with her palm.

(Nadia's pursuing phantom, unabashed, followed directly behind her, and – here was committed a *Grekh* Miriam knew she would never, never later relate – Miriam stooped, and planted her own lips where Nadia had impressed hers.)

Then a surge of émigrés, making obeisances, drove Miriam to a far alcove where a cloth-covered table was laid with neatly classified mail from abroad.

So, Miriam reflected, what better place for Nadia's *Dead Letter Box* than a Russian Church in the heart of London? The name *Nadezhda Stepanovna Cheremisovna* leaped out at her from the cover of a flimsy, faded blue envelope. She withdrew the airmail from the stack and looked for the name of the sender. *Stepan Alexievitch Cheremisov.* She released her suspended breath. *Learn to Interpret by Interpreting*, she thought. Clearly the father was sending his mail to his daughter here at the church, *poste restante*, and not to Leon's flat! Surely that very fact suggested an impermanence in the girl's relations with Leon? Then she softened. Perhaps Nadia feared her father's censure. Perhaps the deception was devised as a propitiation more to confound patriarchal suspicions than Leon's. (Then Miriam saw there was another letter for Nadia – with a London postmark and hastily pencilled address – and abruptly she was not so sure.)

(*Pan.*) Nadia halts on the steps. She removes headscarf as the archpriest departs through side entrance. Looped through his fingers he carries twin gold crowns haloed with sunbeams. Nadia pockets her father's letter, unopened.

(*Reaction shot.*) Miriam's mouth twitches and tightens.

(*Medium closeup.*) Nadia opens letter with London postmark, reads contents, smiles. Applies lipstick. Adjusts sunglasses. Examines watch. Struts towards Knightsbridge.

(*Tracking shot.*) The pursuit was shortlived. Past the Barracks – the air ripe with the sweetness of straw and warm ordure – the two women strolled in the sun. Then they were gone – last seen entering Maxies cocktail bar and restaurant – buried in the traffic blur and wavering fumes. (*Ripple dissolve.*)

(*Mirror shot.*) In the mirror behind the cocktail bar, Nadia could be observed seated at a table talking intently to a young off-duty waiter (or so Miriam judged) – one of London's tribe of hollow-cheeked nightworkers, whose circles of dark flesh beneath the eyes (Miriam noticed on closer inspection) had tautened like blackened drumskins.

Then unbreached custom translated – in a trice – the waiter into diner, for he drew out a chair to seat himself at Nadia's side and waved familiarly to the bar for drinks. Honey Dew Screwdrivers. Vodka, Orange Juice and Melon Liqueur. (Colour? Verdigris green.)

Nadia's companion possessed no discernible earlobes, a certain sign (according to Aunt Wilma) of unregenerate criminality. (Miriam's own lobes were vestigial.)

At the bar, Miriam nibbled from the remains of a dish of *zakuski* – a hint of red and black caviar on toasted roundels – and discovered the waitress, impatient at indecision, had ordered her, unbidden, a Virgin Mary.

(*Closeup.*) At the table, Nadia and her kohl-eyed suitor communed with clasped hands. (*Voiceover,* cigarette-roughened, compelling, "Mais, Nadine, je préfère le vert," etc.)

Miriam drew near, hurrying towards the exit. As she brushed past, her elbow toppled a sugarbowl and fluted glass saltpot. (*Slow motion.*) In the disarray – as the two lovers flailed at the linen cloth – the spilt seasoning was passed from palm to palm. Very soon the lovers began to quarrel and "Nadine" gnawed nervously the ragged ruby chips of her varnished nails.

One last glance at the bar mirror reassured Miriam that any sense of *izlivat dushu* between the couple had now been satisfactorily dispelled.

The Graze

Secure beneath a chainmail of suds, the steam condensing on the ceiling, Miriam searched through veils of mist for the familiars and revenants who at bathtimes would always revisit her.

First she read the star-map of her knees, the pink domes with their constellations of blue grit embedded beneath the skin.

(*Flashback.*) There had been heavy rain. They had gone to the Fair, she, Aunt Wilma and the Old Man – idly following the cinder tracks that had been sprinkled on the sodden turf – until they heard the barker calling them to "The House of Cobwebs". Glimpsing the painted ghouls of the Grand-Guignol, she had struggled to turn back. But the Old Man had held her hand tight, paid ninepence, and drawn her into the dark. Then his hand loosened and he was gone. Too frightened to cry out, she had blundered down the blacked-out maze of passageways, cobwebs brushing her face, banshees screaming from the speakers above, until pulses from a welcoming green light beckoned her on.

Then, in the darkest depths of the corridor, she saw that the light issued from beneath the bearded chin of a gargantuan gargoyle, the green rays fringing its throat, eyes glittering with malevolence. She gazed up in terror. The light turned red and the face erupted into a roar of jubilant laughter. She ran. Stumbled against musty canvas, fumbled for an opening in the tentflap, and, heart pounding with fear, fell upon the cinders.

Aunt Wilma drew the child to her feet, and inspected the plump flesh speckled with fresh blood. The Old Man emerged from the tent, a shamefaced grin buried in his beard. A cold wind sprang up. He hugged his armpits, banging his limbs – a wild semaphore.

(*Still.*) But, face impassive, still Miriam refused to cry.

"No sense no feeling," muttered Aunt Wilma, "the girl has a face like a yard of pump water." But she bent down and whispered, "Bloodied but unbowed, eh? That's right. If the Old Man wants to act the goat there's no call for tears."

The Old Man, soldierly, shrugged deeper into his army trenchcoat and buttoned his upturned collar. He switched off his flashlight with its sliding coloured gels and, stiff-backed, he, too, knelt at her side.

"I was only signalling in the dark," he explained, and held her to him. She clung tightly but felt only the palisade of unrelenting ribbed stays beneath his coat pressed hard against her; until he pulled away, his eyes clouded with pain. Then her tears welled.

The graze.

Children weep for their future lives.
In the cinder grit beneath the skin,
in the nettle's spite and wasp's sting,
apprehend a lover's griefs,
and husband spurned.
And the infant, sobbing,
fallen from her swing,
chants
a lament for wives
abandoned.

(*Flash forward.*) Now, in the bath, tracing again her star-map, she could see the blue flecks had not faded.

(*Flashback.*) That night, Aunt Wilma had sent Miriam to her cot early, unable to outstare the clearsighted, unblinking gaze of the nursery's newborn assessor whose tiny fingers entwined and disengaged so compulsively in the open stitches of a coverlet from which, as she slept, she never withdrew her grasp. When Aunt Wilma switched on the nightlight and padded down the stair the child nestled down and felt for the edge of the blanket. Not until she had performed her comforting ritual of packing a frondlike fringe into one nostril did she sleep.

Later she awoke and heard the Old Man's stockinged feet shuffling on the linoleum as he passed her door to his bedroom. She could hear him muttering, "*Slither 'n' slip to the Land of Counterpane*," and his pillbox rattled in the pocket of his dressing-gown. Only in the very last letter from Aunt Wilma did Miriam learn that his counterpain had been 10 grains of Barbitone rising, in his final years, to a dosage of 30 grains per night.

Next morning, when Miriam opened her eyes she discovered that someone in the night had removed the safety bars of her cot and the pink coverlet with the embroidered letter *M* was gone.

Fifth Report – "The Cherry Orchard"

Despite the changed circumstances between husband and wife, Miriam was reluctant to refuse Leon when he telephoned from the Studios and invited her to roam those vast halls of illusion to view his startling new sets.

When she entered the sound stage she was amazed by the audacity of his vision.

(*Scene. A Forest Track. Night.*) Leon couldn't dissemble his self-applauding grin when he approached to greet her. He pointed to the huge boles of the oak trees, encrusted with lichen, that he had caused to grow in three weeks to the night sky. A dense tangle of branches wove a web on the dark vault above them where electric stars glittered in their courses. Leon buried his finger to the knuckle in the bark of a tree.

"See, they're hot-wire sculptured in polystyrene then sprayed and linked together in sixteen-foot lengths right up to the 'reds'." Leon pointed to the lighting grid – zenith distance – above their heads.

"The sky's a diorama but those branches are real. They're full-grown trees hung upside-down. We bought up an entire cherry orchard in Kent."

Leon described how he had hired 400lb chainwinches to harvest the remains of mature trees – the victims of a hurricane – and how he had assembled a scenedock in the orchard. Now, inside the Studio, the set dressing crew applied the finishing touches.

He nodded towards the director of photography who all morning had been testing a new "swing-and-shift" lens designed to extend his depth of field.

"Remember," Leon said, as the cameraman packed away the 35mm blimped Arriflex, "all the lens sees is the last coat of paint. It's our job to reorchestrate the values of scale to cheat the eye of the camera."

His beard brushed her cheek, and he casually, proprietorially, kissed her temple.

(Under the stars, she thought.)

"The object is to cheat the shot," he said.

When Miriam paused at the exit to glance back at her bearded woodcutter husband at ease within his own sylvan scene – the starlit enchanted forest, the velvet blackness of the painted backcloth – she could not be certain she had not glimpsed a hooded figure clad in dark green moving in the shadows between the trees.

(To see the cherry hung, she thought.)

The Running Noose

(*Resume on interior of Ironmonger's Shop.*) Her speech placid and measured, Miriam bought four yards of three-strand hempen rope and – in an access of secrecy to ensure her visit should pass unremarked – she purchased a number of other needless hardware items.

That night, for the first time, Miriam placed the events of her life in order, as she had promised herself four days before.

(*Flashback.*) They were passing a country churchyard, Aunt Wilma and Miriam (who could not suppose why her aunt had chosen this path). Miriam must have been no more than eleven because she recalled she was wearing her new high school blazer and she remembered its constriction and unaccustomed weight on her back. They walked to an open patch of grass at the far reaches of the graveyard and Aunt Wilma pointed to a plot where there were no headstones.

Later, Miriam had sat on the tomb of the first rector (he was buried with his head to the churchyard wall so on the Day of Resurrection he would be facing his risen flock). Then, immersed in the sickly scent of flowering laurels, she had cried for the mother she had never known.

The Sociogram

Miriam had been taught the techniques of schematics by the Sister Directress. When she examined her own sociogram she saw it conformed in practically all respects to the classic correlative patterns of the classroom most frequently encountered in her textbooks. Leon was without question in the category of class *Star*, forming an exclusive *Mutual Pair* with Nadia, whilst Laurence could be clearly classified a *Rejectee*, leaving Miriam, herself, labelled with the lamedog-tag of *Isolate*, shackled irretrievably in a halter-led, one-way *Chain* of dependence to her father. And, between them, to complete the schema, holding her – as always – at arm's length, stood Aunt Wilma who, though yielding never to her niece, had yet submitted to her station as docile bondservant to the Old Man.

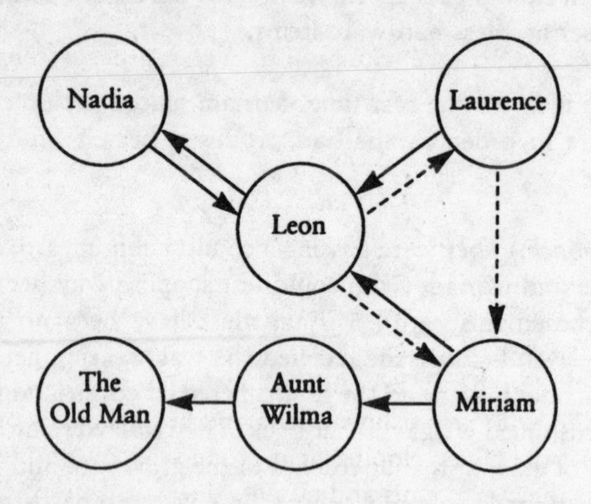

Sixth Report – "Russian Montage"

(*Miriam's Point of View from car parked opposite entrance to Leon's Flat.*) Nadia and Leon emerge and walk away arm in arm.

(*Travelling shot.*) Miriam makes rapid U-turn and parks outside flat entrance.

(*Props note.*) Hempen rope with running noose prominent in view above dashboard.

(*Exterior. Day. Resume on Iron Staircase to Mrs Bryce's Rooftop Flat.*) Sign with arrow points upstairs to *Caretaker.* Old Mrs Bryce limps down staircase. (She labours from the weight of a metal caliper affixed to one ankle, the result of having fallen, two years previously, on treacherous ice on this very staircase.) She wears a patched housecoat; and her crimped hairdo is protected by a faded cotton headscarf. She grunts with satisfaction as she encounters two brand new galvanised zinc buckets placed at the foot of the stairs.

(*Medium closeup.*) Mrs Bryce carries buckets into the Ground Floor rear of Mansion Block.

(*Cut-in . . . extreme closeup.*) A hand attaches hempen noose to wooden crossbar.

(*Découpage in manner of "Russian Montage" cross-cutting on Steps leading to First Floor Flat.*)

(*Cut-in . . .*) The hallway, alcoves and first floor landing are dazzled by a profusion of resplendent *YELLOW FLOWERS*. Bowls, vases, urns are dense with preternaturally glowing blooms.

(*Cut-in . . .*) Mrs Bryce enters from Ground Floor rear, exclaims with astonishment, shaking her head in wonderment at the all-enveloping field of gold, as, muttering, she carries the empty pails and mounts the stairs to First Floor.

(*Cut-in . . . closeup.*) A hand presses steadily on Leon's doorbell.

(*Sustained ringing of bell as automatic door opening device erratically whirs on and off.*)

(*Cut-in . . .*) First Floor Flat door is flung open and Nadia, eyes wide, face pale and distorted with fright, runs to the head of the stairs . . . whirls, as she sees, for the first time, the golden petals that fall across her face. Her fingers describe a crucifix over her mouth.

Nadia:
Svjataja deva Mariya!
(*Subtitles:* **Holy Virgin Mary!**)

(*Cut-in . . .*) Brushing aside the yellow blooms, the old *babushka* Mrs Bryce, breathing heavily, turns a corner of the stairs burdened by the weight of the two buckets.

Nadia:

Poshel k chertu!
Ubiraisya k d'yavolu, staraya ved'ma!
(*Subtitles:* `Go to the Devil! Go to Hell, old witch!`)

(*Cut-in ... extreme closeup.*) Icon of St Nadezhda engulfed in flames.

(*Cut-in ... extreme closeup.*) Nadia screaming.

(*Resume on Steps to Schoolroom Crypt ... Extreme closeup ...*) Little Andrea screaming with infant heartbreak as he stumbles down the stone steps, tears streaming from beneath his wire-framed specs.

(*Softfocus.*) One eye is enlarged and startled behind the lens, the other blind under frosted glass.

The Mancub

(*Interior. Crypt Schoolroom.*) There were no words Miriam could use to comfort the boy. The cardboard box lay empty at his feet. A single black feather drifted across the polished floor. But the bird was gone. How this was so the boy could not know, but he knew he had failed her. He howled at his own betrayal. The other children looked at him with scorn. Miriam gazed at the little mancub, deaf to his imperious rage. (*Lvynok*, Andrea's teacher pronounced to herself, *Little Lion.*) Looking closely, she could see the incipient growth of dark down that furred his cheek along the jawline.

A frost touched her and Miriam allowed the icy crystals to grow around her heart until her resolve was fully made and she was certain she would not soften. Then, since the children had begun to clamour for attention, she restored order by surprising them with a complete change of routine.

Seventh Report – "Unravelling"

(*Interior. Miriam's Fire-lit Study. That night.*) There remained one last task – the destruction of Miriam's "Activities Report"; the removal of the final pages. One by one she tore out the sheets of notes and tossed them on the flames.

(i) *In the Cheremis culture of the Volga–Don region it was believed that the wrath of a saint can be invoked by burning a candle upside-down before its icon.* (The sparkling candles Miriam had lit inverted under the framed print of St Nadezhda had succeeded beyond her modest expectations. A pity Leon's leather Cerrutti had been scorched in the blaze.)

(ii) *An engagement can be prevented by entangling the legs of a table with a rope. Should the girl's father hear of this spell he can break it by chopping both table legs and severing the rope.* (But Stepan Alexievitch Cheremisov had been asleep over two thousand miles away.)

(iii) *An omen of impending misfortune is sight of an old village woman carrying empty pails.* By good fortune loyal Mrs Bryce had sustained only a mild sprain from her second fall. (She had required little prompting to begin the long neglected spring cleaning of the First Floor. As agreed, Miriam had placed the new buckets for collection by the stairs.)

(iv) *When salt is passed from hand to hand these persons quarrel.* True. And the lovers had continued to quarrel shortly after Mrs Bryce had been sent tumbling by Nadia who had jumped into a cab conjured by her kohl-eyed summoner. (*Flashback. Travelling Matte. Taxi Rear Window.*) Nadia sobbed on his shirt-front while he mocked the *ingénue*, but she *had* seen a witch, she *had*, and it would drive her to the Devil. Nadine's quivering finger points to the *ved'ma*, old Mrs Bryce, hobbling after the cab, hurling imprecations.

(v) *The Devil can get in your mouth*. That is why you must make the sign of the cross over your lips.

(vi) *A bird flying into a room is an ill omen*. Andrea's starling had not stirred until Miriam carried the box into Leon's bedroom. She had cradled the tremulous bird in her hands, perching it on the bedside table. Later, when Nadia had entered, the first thing she saw in the candle's flare was a dark fluttering presence like a bat hammering at the window in alarm.

(vii) *Yellow flowers are a sign of infidelity*. Miriam had referred the extract from *The Master and Margarita* to Laurence who had provided an unexpected exegesis of Bulgakov's text which immediately followed the phrase, "*. . . as he whispered he gazed at the moon*." On the telephone she could hear Laurence riffling the pages, then he quoted, "*She was carrying some of those repulsive flowers*," and crowed in recognition. "*It's an ugly colour*," he read, "that's because it's Russki semiotics for an unfaithful woman, it's central to the text, don't you see?" Then she heard a carillon of mordant laughter. "Forgive the emotional histrionicism, but I warned Leon . . ." But Miriam hung up.

She had taken her secateurs and gone straightaway into the garden. First the Yarrow (*Achillea millefolium*) and plumes of Golden Rod, then the yellow Lilies (*Enchantment*), and finally she chose the yellow Aster; not the species plant but the low-bred cultivars that had strayed to the kitchen door – the Aster*asters* – for these she considered the most fitting tribute of all from the philosop*aster*, poet*aster* and ciné*aster* she knew herself to be.

The fire subsided, a flame guttering on the last fragment of paper. The room had grown dark. Miriam switched on the

Old Man's army flashlight (how curious that the dusty *Empire* bulb could function still after remaining inactive for so many years) and a beam of green light was cast on the pink coverlet she had placed on a chair. (*Mise-en-scène.*)

Miriam began to unpick the threads of the blanket, unravelling the pink wool, until she had formed a skein. (To be Penelope at Ithaca, she thought, forever fated to disentangle swaddling clothes to make a shroud.)

In the gloaming, the little dog grew restive on Miriam's lap and leapt in the firelight to the hearth; then, in the singsong voice she reserved for the animal, she crooned:

> *"If I were as pretty as you,*
> *a quarter as pretty would do."*

A ball of wound pink wool rolled from the table edge. (The little white dog **snarled** when the ball reached it. When the little white dog reached it the ball **snarled.**) She must remember, she smiled sleepily, to relate to Laurence this oddity of contextual sensitivity.

From the garden room below Miriam heard Leon's discreet, suppressed sneeze. The sound grated. The truth was that the frequent muffled explosions did, indeed, sound remarkably like *Kissinger!* and, in time, the apprehension as one waited for the next convulsion began to attack one's nerves. (She could glimpse Leon through the glass roof as he poured unsteadily another amber tumbler and the spirit spilled. She was reminded that tomorrow the first lesson was an exercise in *differential visual-tacticle-muscular perception of form.*)

She stepped out onto the terrace above the garden room and in her peripheral vision she had a prickling sense of the planets teeming above her. She stared up at the overarching night. She whispered as she gazed at the crescent moon which appeared to her as the half-closed stopper of a dark urn in which she had been irredeemably entombed and the scattering of stars seemed to her as light dimly penetrating the filigree of an abandoned design; fragments of an unfinished frieze chased on the outer surface of her sepulchre. Yet what the subject of the original pattern could have been – strain her eyes as she might – she could not possibly begin to guess.

Ocarina

Louise Doughty

Somehow or other, light must have dawned. Sometime after the ocarina.

Perhaps it was on that coach trip, yes, that coach trip down to London.

We had argued. Before I had stormed out of his house, I had managed to let him know that I would be just in time to catch the 6.45 from St George's bus station. As I stood queueing for my ticket, it seemed inconceivable that he would not be charging round the inner ring road in his Mini, cursing the other drivers in a desperate attempt to get to the station on time. As Express Service no. 737 pulled into the station, it seemed impossible that he would not be racing up the slope from the car park, his coat flapping open and his scarf flying in the wind. As I handed over my ticket and looked around for a free seat in the smoking section, it was out of the question that he would not materialise in front of the vehicle and threaten to hurl himself under its wheels unless I dismounted, embraced him and swore to stay by his side forever.

I would have to apologise to the driver. The other passengers would smile at each other and shake their heads indulgently. A granny would turn to a companion and sigh, nostalgically, "Ah . . . young lovers . . . I don't know . . ." Then, as the coach pulled away, we would be left in each other's arms on the pavement, our faces pressed together, oblivious to the rain that trickled down our necks.

Even as the coach hit the motorway, as I wriggled in my

seat to find the comfiest position, I pictured how we would walk back to his car, arm in arm, to discover that he had been given a parking ticket. As the theme tune began, he would pull it from the wiper, look at it, grin and tear it into two. The final shot, as the credits rolled, would be of the car pulling away, followed by a closeup of the ticket in the gutter, carelessly discarded.

I think it was when we pulled into Luton that it occurred to me that none of this was going to happen.

My father took my return with his usual toad-like stoicism. We sat in front of the television, holding newspapers to fend each other off. Aunt banged saucers and cups together in the kitchen.

"How's work?"

"All right. Busy."

He turned a page. "Your Aunt gets worse every day. How's college?"

"Well, it isn't really a college." We have this discussion every time I come home. It's all one and the same to him; the WEA Photography Workshop I go to once a week, universities, polytechnics, the primary school I teach at, the lot. We are paper men and women living in paper houses. We eat paper. We shit paper. My father spent most of his life on street corners selling the *Evening Standard*. His dislike of us is one of the few things about him I respect.

Aunt bustles in with her apron still tied around her bulging middle. Her wig is slightly askew and she is smiling. She goes over to the fire and stabs at it a few times with the poker, kneeling on one knee. Old age has been kind to my aunt in a way that youth and my father were not. It has given her nothing – but then she expected nothing and had not been disappointed. She picks up the brass tongs, then leans over and sees that the bucket is empty.

"Whatever did we do before coal?" she mutters happily into the fire. She leaves.

"Found yourself a young lady yet then?" Dad asks spitefully. I don't reply, by which I mean to indicate that I am onto him. It won't work. I refuse to be needled. He grunts at my silence. "Not getting any younger you know. Lad like you." (I am twenty-five.)

"No, Dad." I reply, as a concession to his age. I must have been very young when I worked out that the best way to handle those who had reared you was to sigh, agree and ignore. It was no doubt taught to me by Forster or the Bible or some other bit of paper – books that are full of people who have survived because of the things they have left unsaid. Not only have they survived but they have been the moral victors. I am superior to my father in intelligence, education and social awareness but I still need to feel, every now and then, that I am the one who has the strength to back down in an argument.

Aunt comes back in with the coal. When she has finished stoking the fire and cleaning up the dishes, she will start on the ironing. It is nearly eleven o'clock at night. She will be up at five. Monday is her early shift at the nursing home where she cleans up after people two, three, five years older than herself. My father is eight years younger.

"Why don't you have work this week then?" she says to me over her shoulder as she picks up the lumps of coal, one by one, and places them on the fire with infinite care.

"Half term." I know she would like more details but I am tired and bad-tempered. Ever since I started at the school, in September, I have been promising I will bring her pictures of the children, eight-year-olds. Nothing pleases her more, during my infrequent visits home, than anecdotes about little Leo or Marina or Jamie. When I told her that the father of one of my class was a pilot for British Airways, her wig nearly stood on end. "Fancy. Our Harry," she said, as if I had been knighted.

I remember reading somewhere that misogynists are often born of women who do everything for husbands who are lazy or brutal or alcoholic. The boy-child despises his mother for not standing up to the father, for not changing him. In his turn, the child also becomes lazy or brutal or alcholic or any combination of the three. I am far from a misogynist but I don't love my Aunt (as we call her, euphemistically). Perhaps if she had not stepped in where my mother left off, when I was very small, perhaps my father would have realised how emotionally corrupt he is. If she had not looked after me, perhaps he would have had to. Then there is the uncomfortable fact that her devotion demonstrates that even he is lovable. So how do I excuse my own disgust when I see his yellow teeth or dirty handkerchiefs or smell him?

I am bad. I have always been bad. I have failed to love my father, string vests, varicose veins, foul breath and all. He has never read a book. I am the failure.

"Oh yes, half term," my Aunt informs the glowing embers. A spark flies into her lap and she jumps up and shakes her apron. My father does not move.

All at once, I can't stand to be in the room with either of them. "I'll put the kettle on."

In the kitchen, faced with my own reflection in the window, I am nauseous with loneliness. I fill the tin kettle and put it on the left hand gas ring, at the back, the only one that works properly.

The kitchen hasn't changed. Tatty net curtains drape from a wire strung halfway up the window. Cast-iron pots and pans are hung on the wall in order of descending size. Special offer tumblers are ranged upside-down on the chequered formica. Suds sit in bubbles round their rims. A teatowel with an authentic recipe for Yorkshire pudding lies discarded over the back of a badly painted kitchen chair.

There is cutlery in the drainer. Aunt was only halfway through the drying-up when it occurred to her that the fire might be getting low.

He hasn't even phoned.

I had sex with a woman once. In the middle of it, a noise

began. It wasn't a normal noise, a banging or a squelching or anything like that. It was a sort of intermittent squealing, like a bicycle braking very suddenly or a piglet in pain. Her fingers were entwined in my hair and the back of my neck was running with sweat. I sneaked a look at her face but her eyes and mouth were tight shut. I slowed down, and the noise became less frequent. I speeded up again and so did the noise. There was no doubt about its source. It was *down there*.

I couldn't stand it any longer. My erection died. I shuddered a little, half-heartedly, and then withdrew. Every part of my body was moist except one. I fumbled with the condom so that I wouldn't have to look at her.

She was a friend. We were both second-years on the primary B.Ed course. We shared the notes we took in lectures. She was nice. I liked her. She was messing around with tissues so that she didn't have to look at me. All I could think about was tomorrow's practical lesson, on potato printing, and how we had agreed to share King Edwards.

We both lay back on the bed, side by side. Getting our clothes back on was going to be even more awkward and embarrassing than getting them off had been. I wondered who would be the first to speak.

"It wasn't your fault," she said suddenly. "They did warn me at the clinic." I looked at her. "Well I've only just got the cap you see, I didn't want to fill myself with hormones and I thought it was best. It's just, well, I've only had it for a few days, to practise putting it in and they said if I had sex I had to use something else as well until they've checked I'm doing it right that's why I made you wear . . . they did warn me." She propped her head up with one hand and plucked at the pillow with the other. "They did say the two . . . rubber surfaces might make a squeaking noise.

I live in a small flat on the main road that leads into the town centre. I like living on my own. My rent is cheap and I eat vegetables and feel self-sufficient and hermetic. Extract from my diary just after I moved in: "I can't imagine ever bringing a lover back to this flat." Every now and then I get stoned. I eat fromage frais under the influence and imagine myself to be subversive. I pretend I am living in one of those novels about pale young men who fool the world that they are quiet little teachers or librarians or bank clerks – until they write or paint their masterpieces. The world is shocked.

I don't write or paint anything. Most of my eight-year-olds have more artistic sensibility than me. I like taking photographs and I go to a workshop every Wednesday evening to try and learn how to do it properly. That is how I met Martin.

Martin knows how to do it properly. He's even sold a couple of things. In between, he sells advertising space on the local newspaper. He's good at it, I think, good at telling people why they should spend their money in that particular way and what profits it will bring them. Martin's favourite saying is: *there is no such thing as a free drink*. He is strong. He likes macaroni cheese. He is careless. He goes through phases of humming the same tune, over and over again, for weeks at a time. When I first met him it was *Life Upon the Wicked Stage*. He is of medium height and medium build. Physically, everything about him is medium, except his smile which, as all the best smiles tend to, claims you. There is something innately proprietorial about the way he glances at you. You feel exhausted when he looks away. There is no fooling Martin, not that man.

Once, early on in the relationship, we were sitting outside a café in town. It was one of those new continental-style things with white tables and chairs under huge coloured umbrellas. We had just passed the stage when you think that the person you have met is perfect. We were re-adjusting ourselves. To make it less awkward, I was talking about the people sitting around us. (A week before we would have been playing footsie under the table.) I pointed out a man and said he was a lawyer. Martin spotted a chemical engineer. Then he said, "Look at those three."

He motioned with his spoon to where a man and two women were sitting. The man was in his mid-forties, impeccably dressed, with an alert, hard air about him. He was giving orders to the waiter without lifting his head from the menu. Sitting next to him, close up, was a woman in her early thirties, dressed in a navy suit and court shoes, legs crossed, with her hair piled on top of her head and a clutch bag on the table in front of her.

She was watching the man's every move, his face as he spoke, his hands as he gestured. Every now and then, she patted the back of her head, to make sure her hair was still in place.

The other woman was in her early to mid-twenties. She was dressed in trousers and a cheap, trendy jacket. She looked out of place in the café. She would have been more at home in a pub, smart but with a pool table.

The waiter returned with a pot of tea and three cups. The man distributed the cups and then picked up the pot. The older woman was still gazing at him. Leaning forward over the table, he poured tea for the younger. Immaculate cuffs protruded from his jacket sleeve and square gold cufflinks caught the sun. As he finished, he leaned over the table and said something to her softly, at her face. She looked down into her tea and fiddled with her spoon. Only when he had finished speaking did he straighten himself and serve the older woman, who still stared at him ceaselessly, wearing a plastic smile and talking, talking, talking.

"See them," said Martin, "now shall I tell you about them?" I watched them, the younger one's discomfort, the woman's panic and the man's self-assurance. "He is a businessman, mid-forties, successful, hard-working and still on his way up. In five years' time he will have peaked and they'll make him redundant but he doesn't know it yet. At the moment, he has everything. She is his mistress, the one with all the hair. Perhaps she is a personal assistant or something or perhaps they just met somewhere but either way, it's a long-standing relationship. Several years. When they met, she was on the up and up as well but she doesn't care about that now. All she cares about is him. Him, his money and his status, but mostly him. He has taught her to do that. He has made things turn out the way he wanted. The other one, the cute one, she is a friend of the mistress. Perhaps she's a younger sister. She's a bit scared of him but sort of titillated in a way. He's different from boys her own age and it is funny and new to have someone buy you drinks and things. Guess what's going to happen?" I shook my head. "Well he is going to make a pass at the young one of course, that's why he has manipulated her into joining them. Maybe in a few weeks, maybe months, but sooner or later. The other one knows it and she's absolutely terrified."

I looked at Martin, then back at the other table. "What will happen?"

"Well it all depends on the missy there. She might be so embarrassed she accepts in which case he will hang onto both of them and have a good time until he gets caught. When that happens, the older one will take an overdose or something and the two women will never speak to each other again. If the younger one has any sense, she'll give him a grand speech about loyalty and turn him down, in which case he'll ditch the other and go after something completely different."

"Sounds like the older one has a rough time either way," I commented, trying to sound intelligent and detached, like him.

He frowned at me. "But that's not the point. The point is, it's all about power. People and everything. It's all about power."

That was nearly a year ago now, that conversation, and I must have known even then. It was some months later that I gave Martin Wilson a present, an ocarina.

I had chosen it specially from amongst the others on a

market stall. I had gone to wander one Saturday morning. I couldn't bear the peace and quiet of my flat any longer. They were collected in a wicker basket, hawked by a hunched old man with a crab-apple face and a gloomy fringe hanging down over his forehead. There was a crowd round the stall. He was demonstrating, blowing into the tiny hole at the top. Out of his wizened lips and through his cracked fingers came stinging little notes, higher than those of a flute and less civilised, loose and anarchic – pagan. I was enraptured.

The ocarinas came complete with leather thongs and a note on their origins, conjuring up visions of Iceni warriors and bleak, windswept, pre-Christian hillsides. They came in different glazes, browns and greys. The customers were poking around for ones they liked, while the old man played and searched us with his eyes. "It's for our daughter," the couple in front of me explained as they bought theirs.

I imagined telling him sheepishly, "It's for my 47-year-old lover."

My 47-year-old lover turned it over in his hand and said, "What's it for?"

I had chosen the wrong time to give it to him. He had just come back from seeing his wife and he was always bad-tempered after he had seen her. But even so. I had wrapped it up, in tissue paper, and bought one of those do-it-yourself boxes. I thought it would catch his imagination. He was going through an ethnic phase at the time, hanging rugs on his walls and buying compact discs of lute music.

"It's an ocarina," I protested feebly.

"Yes," he said, "but what's it *for*?"

When we first met, he would look at me so hard and with such depth my head would grow light. I could almost forget I had a body at all. I had never met anyone so careful and attentive. There is no aphrodisiac quite like being wanted very badly – and there is no pain quite like its sudden withdrawal.

❦

I remember a friend once saying to me that what made her leave her lover was seeing her parents holding hands while they were watching the nine o'clock news. It showed her just how Good and Honest and True a relationship could be. I wish I could say the same. I wish I could say that as I went back into the sitting-room my father was standing with his hand on Aunt's shoulder, or that he was helping her to brush down her apron – that they were exchanging a look or a word; just something small, small but redemptive.

As I went in, Aunt rose and took the tray from my hands and put it on the coffee table. She poured the drinks. They trickled in the silence.

Dad was still stuck behind his paper, like a monument or monarch. The ends of his fingers were yellow. The tap dripped in the kitchen and my father's breathing was hoarse and heavy and even. Aunt sighed.

"You were talking about leaving the school last time you were home," she said softly, without looking up.

I had talked of it, talked of moving back to London. It would mean leaving Martin. I sipped at my drink, watching Aunt's arthritic hands.

There is such a thing as a free drink, you know. My Aunt is free, not in the sense of being unchained but in the sense of giving herself without expectation. She is a dense, heavy woman, but she is free.

"I don't know," I reply, sipping at my drink again and hearing Dad's motiveless breathing and the tap dripping and the crackling of the fire. "I don't know."

The Drawing Room

Clare Girvan

Lucy is at the window of Fairwinds, looking in. It is night and the new electric lamps show the Talbots in their drawing room. The lamps have little pink shades and cast posies of light onto the rugs and ceiling. In Lucy's own house one cream-shaded bulb hung from the centre serves each room with a bright, flat light. Her mother says she wants to be able to see what she is doing.

Auntie Rose is knitting. Uncle Alfred is reading. Flora and Bertie are lying on the rug with a jigsaw puzzle between them. Bundle is curled round like a Danish pastry, pressing into the warm fender. Baby Tom sleeps upstairs in his cradle, nurse dozing in an armchair. This is how the Talbots spend all their evenings, waiting for her.

Lucy loves the Talbots and visits them secretly so that her mother will not find out. Lucy's mother says the Talbots are "well-heeled". They have a cook and a kitchen maid who wear white caps and live in the basement, and a neat housemaid who sits on a chair in the hall. Lucy loves Fairwinds too, because it has high ornamental gables, sea-shells round the front door and lace curtains at all the windows. She loves to go from room to room, up and down the wide central staircase, seating herself elegantly on the red padded chairs like a lady, examining the framed seascapes on the walls and the tiny model ship in a bottle, stroking the smooth fruit in the bowls, peeping into Captain Talbot's study, tip-toeing into the nursery to see if Baby

Tom is awake. But she loves it most because the Talbots are there.

Lucy's mother is very particular about Fairwinds. "That house belonged to my grandmother," she says. "It's an heirloom, and you'll only go and break something if you play with it all the time."

But Lucy never does play with it. She doesn't need to.

The front of the house is hinged so that it swings open to reveal the whole of the inside, but Lucy never likes to expose the Talbots in this way, and waits till they see her and call her in to sit down by their fire.

"Ah, Lucy," Captain Talbot says. "Just in time for a song." And he sits down at the piano, waves his hands in the air, and plunges into "Daisy, Daisy." Captain Talbot is tall and handsome and has a big, curly, sailor's beard. He only ever sings "Daisy, Daisy."

"Lucy, dear, how nice," Mrs Talbot says. "Would you be a pet and hold my wool for me? Flora and Bertie say that can't leave their puzzle."

"It's a difficult bit, Mama," Flora says. "We'll help in a moment."

But they leave it to Lucy, who perches happily on the stool, tilting her hands, watching the wool slip backwards and forwards, watching Auntie Rose winding the ball of wool bigger and bigger, her hands going faster and faster until all her fingers are whirling together and her sparkly ring is like a saraband of stars. Auntie Rose is beautiful. She wears a high-collared lace blouse with big sleeves, and her hair in waves piled up high on her head. Lucy sometimes thinks she looks like Mother from *The Railway Children*. Her smile is as soft as velvet and she sits like a mermaid on a rock, trawling the sea with her wool, her eyes as close as shells.

"I can't afford a carriage!" sings Captain Talbot.

"Lucy!"

The name mingles with the rhythm and is lost.

"Lucy!" Sharper, rising through the melody. Captain Talbot stops, his head on one side.

"Hark. Do I hear a voice?"

"Got to go and have my tea, Auntie Rose," Lucy whispers.

"That's right." Mrs Talbot nods, smiles. Her eyes open luminously. "You're a growing girl. Off you go. Come and see us later."

The irritable voice is insistent.

"Lucy! It's pitch dark and your egg's getting cold. What are you doing up there?"

"Nothing."

Lucy opens the bedroom door and light spills in, making her eyes water. In the hall below, her mother's red mouth still works angrily at her wasted words and the equally wasted words of the television argue back at her. She does not like silence, so it stays on all the time, whether anyone is watching it or not. On the screen a child flounders in a creek and is rescued by a dog and reunited with his family. Lucy sits on the sofa next to her mother in an identical attitude, plate on her lap, eyes on the television, slowly dipping strips of toast into the congealing egg. A string of yolk dribbles down her front.

"Look what you're doing." Her mother does not look away from the screen. Lucy scrapes at her dress with toast. "Put that in the wash when you've finished. As if I haven't got enough to do."

The news begins. Lucy takes a piece of cake and picks at the top.

"Don't do that," her mother says. "How many times have I told you?"

"I don't like walnuts," Lucy says.

"Give them to me then."

Lucy eats the cake silently, with equal bites. Her mother nips bits off the walnuts with her front teeth.

"Can I go and play now?"

"Go on then. Don't make a noise. And only one light

out there," she adds, hearing the click of two switches. "You don't have to pay the bills."

The landing light makes a safe cave, and she scuttles up the stairs before the tiger at the bottom can realise that the hall is dark and come growling out after her. At the top the stairs curve round, leading to the light and safety.

She puts her dress in the wicker basket in the bathroom and stands in her slip to see if she has grown tall enough yet to see into the mirror over the wash basin. But only the top of her head shows, with the bow that ties back her hair in its fashionable plait.

Turning sideways, she can dimly discern her tubby little body reflected in the dark green wall tiles. They are nice tiles, decorated with a curving pink lily in a corner of each. For a few minutes she ducks and twirls, holding out the edge of her slip and pointing her toes as she has learned in ballet class. She is not good at ballet. She is too heavy and does not bend gracefully in the middle like the other girls. But the faint, gleaming figure on the wall drifts lightly among the lilies in the green depths of the tiles like a nymph of the sea, far, far down in the weedy reaches of the Sargasso. Her arms are long and lovely fronds, rippling out over the tides. She thinks of Auntie Rose.

The volume of sound downstairs increases as the sitting room door opens. Quickly she tugs out the light and skips across the landing to her bedroom.

She taps the bars of the hamster cage, but James is hidden under a heap of mangled tissues. He is not a very good pet; he cannot be cuddled or trained, and although he seems to know her, he is not affectionate. She would like a dog like Bundle, but her mother has said no.

It is not time for bed yet, but she takes her pyjamas out of the furry cat case on the bed. He looks starved without them, so she stuffs him with her rolled-up slip and socks and arranges him in a languid loll on the pillow. His wobbly eyes have settled crossed, so she gives him a little shake to straighten them.

Outside it is night, the topsy-turvy time of year, when you get up in the dark, and in no time at all it is dark again for tea. The world turns to make day and night; it hates the cold and rushes to get it over, then dawdles through the warm days to make it last. They had read a poem about it at school.

"In winter I get up at night and dress by yellow candle-light," she murmurs against the window-pane. The moon is coming up early over the rooftops, beginning to probe and peer in at the windows. Soon it will travel across the room, searching out corners, missing nothing.

Her breath makes the glass misty, hiding her from its pale, supercilious eye. She draws a squiggle, lets it trickle down, and wonders what it would be like to have to use candles to see by. To go upstairs only protected by a pool of candlelight must be the worst thing in the world; shadows would rear up behind and before you, making you drip hot wax, and the moon would pursue you through the window and tell the tiger where you were.

A key in the front door. Her father, home from work. She creeps out and sits on the top stair. He was in a bad temper this morning, but perhaps he isn't angry any more. If he isn't, she will be able to go down. She listens.

Fragments of talk, confused by the television. The familiar, querulous wail of her mother's voice rising. The staccato note of her father's irritation. An ugly trio of voices, prowling the hallway, stealing up the stairs, waking the tiger, retreating.

A couple of tears drop down onto the carpet, and she rubs them into the curly pattern with her finger. Soon her mother will be crying too, then her father will become angry again and slam out of the room or even out of the house, and Lucy will have to stay awake until he comes back, otherwise he won't come back at all. Sometimes, if it is a really bad row, her mother shouts that she is going to cut her wrists, and her father shouts back "Good!"

Lucy clenches her bottom tightly, then crosses her thumbs and folds her fingers over them, hard, so that her mother won't shout it. If she does, there will be days of silent breakfasts, and Lucy will be afraid to go to school and leave her, and afraid to come home again in the afternoon, in case she has done the awful thing she threatens to do, and it will be Lucy's fault for going to school and letting her.

But all is quiet and she unlaces her fingers and gets to her feet, wiping her nose on her pyjama sleeve. It is cold on the landing. She rubs a foot against her leg, wishing she had worn her slippers.

James wakes up and scrabbles frantically round in his wheel. Lucy puts some more food into his dish and goes across to Fairwinds. The drawing room lamps are on and the fire burns in the grate. Tea is laid in the dining room, five chairs drawn up. There is enough for twenty; a pink hambone, a castle of blancmange, jam tarts, a glazed cottage loaf, butter, four plates of sandwiches, a green jelly, a rose-painted tea pot, milk in white jug, a wedge of cheese, a cake spotted with currants, a bowl of fruit. Jane the maid waits at the sideboard.

"Goodness," cries Mrs Talbot on seeing Lucy. "You've been crying, my dear. Now come and tell Auntie Rose what's wrong."

Lucy runs to bury her head in the silken lap, and Mrs Talbot strokes her hair, murmuring like an incantation. Flora and Bertie watch with round eyes.

"Just feel your little feet," Mrs Talbot goes on. "Frozen solid. Alfred, my love, bring that stool up to the fire and let the poor child get warm."

Captain Talbot presents the stool with a bow.

"Madame," he says with deep respect. "Allow me." Lucy giggles and he folds her feet into his lovely big warm hands. Mrs Talbot chafes the blood back into her fingers. Her palms whisper with the rubbing, and the sparkly ring flashes. Warmth seeps through Lucy's veins, her eyelids drowse down.

"I know just the thing for chilly feet," announces Uncle Alfred. "How about a thoroughly rousing game of Blind Man's Buff?"

"Oh, yes, yes!" shout Flora and Bertie, startling Lucy awake again. "Daddy will be Blind Man, won't you, Daddy?"

Uncle Alfred laughingly agrees, and Auntie Rose hurries to move vases.

Uncle Alfred is a wonderful Blind Man. Lucy is sure he can see and accuses him of cheating, but he immediately bumps into Flora and falls over the stool to prove that he isn't. He makes wild grabs at the air, so that everyone has to dodge out of his way. Even Bundle joins in, barking and jumping up.

Uncle Alfred catches Lucy and holds her upside-down, pretending he cannot guess who she is, and she squeals with delight.

Suddenly the game stops. Everything is as still as rocks.

"Quick," says Lucy. "Mum's coming."

She reaches her bedroom just as her mother bursts in. She is breathless and red-faced.

"Why on earth are you in your pyjamas? Get dressed quickly. We're going out."

"Going out?" Lucy repeats.

"You heard. I'll pack while you get dressed. You can wear your school uniform. We'll get the rest later."

"Where are we going?" Lucy does not move.

"To Auntie Phyl's." Her mother begins throwing shoes and clean underwear into a case.

"Why are we?"

"Just for a holiday. It's all arranged."

"But why? Is Dad coming?" She knows the answer before it is given.

"Dad's staying here. We're leaving."

"Leaving Dad? But how long for?"

"For good. We're never coming back to this house again. You can take your hamster and one or two of your toys with you if you want. There's no room for anything else. Don't just stand there, Luce. I'm in a hurry."

"But I can't – " Lucy tries to say. Her mother pauses.

"Look, Luce, we're just going away, that's all. Now, you get dressed while I go and collect my things." She hurries out. Lucy hears her banging drawers next door.

"Auntie Rose," she cries, running into the drawing room. "Mum says I've got to go away and never come back."

Her tears soak into Mrs Talbot's pretty tucked blouse. She draws Lucy down to the floor in front of her. Her face is shadowed against the pink lamps and her weight of hair is loose over her shoulders. The light gleams through it as she bends forward. Lucy is engulfed by the sweet-scented fall of hair. She wants to drown in it.

"There, my dear, nobody shall take you anywhere if you don't want to go." Auntie Rose's voice is lilting and low, almost singing. Over and over she says it, No one shall take you if you don't want to go.

"Stay, Lucy," Flora says. "You can share my room. It'll be such fun to have a sister. Please, Daddy, tell her to stay."

"Lucy must decide," says Uncle Alfred.

Bertie joins in. "Don't go, Lucy. You can play with Bundle whenever you like."

They surround her, Uncle Alfred, Auntie Rose, Flora, Bertie. Their voices mingle; they croon, they console, No one shall take you, Please stay, Lucy must decide. Their hands nibble at her like the tiny mouths of fish. Auntie Rose's ring flares brighter than ever as if a draught has caught it; Lucy can hardly take her dazzled eyes off it. The figures blur and the voices wrap her around until she is floating in a warm swaddle of bands as soft as Auntie Rose's hair. Lucy must decide.

She gets up stiffly. The hands fall gently away and she walks into the hall. Jane settles her little white cap on her head and smiles.

"You going out, Miss Lucy?"

"I don't know," Lucy replies.

Once, when younger, she looked down the wrong end of a telescope and saw the world from a dizzying distance, unreachably far. She had laughed because however much she stretched she could not touch it, and felt a strange pleasure at the unoccupied space between herself and the diminished world at the end.

From the doorway she can see her bedroom quite clearly in its bland light. The moon, outdone, shines dully behind the window, as insignificant as a cracked plate. From far away she can see a bed with a blue quilt and furry cat, a shelf of dolls, a hamster in a cage, a small desk and matching chair, a few books. They do not belong to her, but to another child, another time. She is still swathed in the soft bands. They are loose and comfortable; they will be off at the merest twitch. One foot is already over the doorsill.

From the next room her mother calls, "Lucy, are you ready yet? The taxi will be here in a minute."

She is too late. Lucy decides.

"I'm ready. Thank you, Jane."

The bands float away, away. She is as light as sea foam now.

The Talbots hold out their arms. Lucy walks back into Fairwinds. Jane closes the door behind her.

About the Authors

Kate Atkinson
Won the Whitbread Book of the Year Award with her first novel, *Behind the Scenes at the Museum*, which is set in York, where she was born. Her career began when she won a *Woman's Own* short story competition. Her new book, *Human Croquet*, was published in March 1997.

Cari Crook
Teaches children with special needs, and now works part time in order to write. She has had several stories published in magazines and says she is attracted by "dark fantasy and crime". She lives in Leicester.

Cathy Cullis
Has been writing poetry for a number of years, and won the Society of Authors' Eric Gregory Award for her work. She was inspired to begin writing fiction after a trip to Arizona in 1996. She lives with her husband in Hampshire.

Rachel Cusk
Won the Whitbread First Novel Award in 1993 with *Saving Agnes* and has also written *The Temporary*. She has had numerous short stories published and writes regularly for various newspapers. Her new book, *The Country Life*, was published in May 1997. She lives in London.

Olivia Davison
Works as a lawyer on the Derbyshire border and has been studying for an MA in creative writing at Nottingham Trent University for the past two years. Her stories are inspired by the years she spent as a criminal lawyer.

Louise Doughty
Shot into the bestseller list with her first novel, *Crazy Paving*, and followed this last year with another hit, *Dance with Me*. She has won various awards for her short stories and is now a regular reviewer and broadcaster. Her new book, *Honey-dew*, will be published in January 1998.

Catherine Eisner
Divides her time between Sussex and West Africa, where her husband heads a trade mission. She donated her prize money from the Asham Award to a technical school in Ghana to help them buy equipment.

Layn Feldman
Began writing after her father died and in her stories she captures the voice of her parents – the children of Russian-Jewish émigrés. This is her first story to be published and is part of a collection, inspired by her family, entitled *Letting Go Slowly*. She has a degree in psychology and lives in London.

Ann Gilchrist
Is a probabation officer in Hampshire but has been writing "ever since I could hold a pen". Whilst working in Tanzania for Voluntary Service Overseas she began a correspondence course in creative writing. *The Sign* was inspired by the mix of magic and reality which she found in East Africa.

Clare Girvan
Retired from primary school teaching last year to devote more time to writing. She and her husband live near Exeter, where she belongs to a writing group. This is her second story to win a prize.

Susan Holland
Lives in London and is researching 19th century literature at City University. She began taking her writing seriously about nine years ago and has won several awards. The story in this anthology is inspired by childhood, but she says her inspiration comes from many different images and emotions, both positive and negative, which make up everyday life.

Leila Keys
Was born in India and now practises as a psychiatrist in London. She always wanted to write, and eventually joined a creative writing group and has been writing seriously for about two years. Many of her stories are concerned with "belonging".

Candia McWilliam
Winner of the Guardian Fiction Prize 1994 and author of *A Case of Knives*, *A Little Stranger* and *A Debatable Land*. She has three children and lives in Oxford.

Deborah Moggach
Has written numerous novels, the most recent being *The Ex-Wives* and *Seesaw.* She also writes for stage and TV, and won an award for her screenplay *Goggle-Eyes*. She has written two collections of short stories and her new book *Close Relations* was published in March 1997.

Anne Summerfield
Has written for most of her life, and worked in computers before deciding to study for a PhD in contemporary women's short stories. She belongs to a writing group in Hampshire and is married with two children.

Erica Wagner
Came to live in London from New York about ten years ago and works as literary editor of *The Times*. She has had a number of short stories published and is married to a writer.

Nargis Walker
Was born in Aden, educated in India and now lives with her husband and two children in Sussex, where she teaches English at a Sixth Form College. She came to writing "almost by accident" whilst studying for an MA. This story, her first to be published, was one of the assignments on her course.

Julia Widdows
Lives with her husband and two sons in Sussex and works in special education. She has been "writing forever" but this is her first story to be published. It was inspired, she says, by her fascination for the images of life seen through lighted windows.